COME CLOSER

Sara Gran is the author of six critically acclaimed novels, including the Claire DeWitt series. She also writes for film and TV, including *Southland* and *Chance*, and has published in the *New York Times*, the *New Orleans Times Picayune* and *USA Today*.

Further praise for *Come Closer*:

'*Come Closer* is riveting, alarming, and deceptively complex. Sara Gran will make you terrified of the little voice lurking inside your own mind that sometimes says, *Go ahead, do it*.' **Madeline Stevens**

'Short, sharp and deliciously, remorselessly nasty; I read it in one compulsive gulp while trying to ignore the slow chills creeping up and down my spine.' **Lucy Caldwell**

'Stunning.' *Los Angeles Review of Books*

'One of the signal works of contemporary female horror.' *New York Times*

'About as twisted as they come.' *CrimeReads*

'What begins as a sly fable about frustrated desire evolves into a genuinely scary novel about possession and insanity.

Hypnotic, disturbing, and written with such unerring confidence you believe every word.' **Bret Easton Ellis**

'A perfectly noirish tale of madness and love. Author Sara Gran writes with scalpel-like clarity, expertly blending tones to create a new kind of psychological thriller. I loved this book. Days after finishing it, it has not left my mind.' **George Pelecanos**

'*The Yellow Wallpaper* meets *Rosemary's Baby* in a slim, wonderfully eerie novel.' *Kirkus*

'This ambiguous balancing of the psychological and supernatural creates just the right amount of narrative tension to keep the reader turning pages ... Gran demonstrates that an urbane and subtle approach to ideas more often treated with hysteria and flash can still produce a gripping contemporary tale of terror.' *Publishers Weekly*

COME CLOSER

SARA GRAN

faber

First published in the USA in 2003
by Soho Press, Inc.

First published in the UK in 2005
by Atlantic Books

This edition published in the UK in 2021
by Faber & Faber Ltd
Bloomsbury House
74–77 Great Russell Street
London WC1B 3DA

Typeset by Faber & Faber Ltd
Printed and bound by CPI Group (UK) Ltd, Croydon CR0 4YY

A CIP record for this book
is available from the British Library

ISBN 978-0-571-35555-6

MIX
Paper from
responsible sources
FSC® C020471

10 9 8 7 6 5 4 3 2 1

For Warren and Suzanne Gran.
Thank you for everything.

I n January I had a proposal due to my boss, Leon
Fields, on a new project. We were renovating a clothing
store in a strip mall outside the city. Nothing tremendous. I finished the proposal on a Friday morning and
dropped it on his desk with a cheerful little note—"Let
me know what you think!"—while he was in a meeting
with a new client in the conference room.

Later that morning Leon threw open his office door
with a bang.

"Amanda!" he called. "Come in here."

I rushed to his office. He picked up a handful of papers
off his desk and stared at me, his flabby face white with
anger.

"What the hell is this?"

"I don't know." It looked like my proposal—same
heading, same format. My hands shook. I couldn't
imagine what was wrong. Leon handed me the papers
and I read the first line: *Leon Fields is a cocksucking
faggot.*

"What is this?" I asked Leon.

He stared at me. "You tell me. You just dropped it on
my desk."

My head spun. "What are you talking about? I put the proposal on your desk, not this, the proposal for the new job." I sifted through the papers on his desk for the proposal I had dropped off. "What is this, a joke?"

"Amanda," he said. "Three people said they saw you go to the printer, print this out, and bring it to my desk."

I felt like I had stepped into a bad dream. There was no logic, no reason anymore. "Wait," I said to Leon. I ran back to my desk, printed out the proposal, checked it, and brought it back to Leon's office. He had calmed down a little and was sitting in his big leather chair.

I handed it to him. "This is it. This is exactly what I put on your desk this morning."

He looked over the papers and then looked back up at me. "Then where did *that* come from?" He looked back at the fake proposal on the desk.

"How would I know?" I said. "Let me see it again."

I read the second line: *Leon Fields eats shit and likes it.*

"Disgusting," I said. "I don't know. Someone playing a trick on you, I guess. Someone thinks it's funny."

"Or playing a trick on *you*," he said. "Someone replaced your proposal with this. I'm sorry, I thought—" he looked around the office, embarrassed. In the three years I had worked for him I had never heard Leon Fields apologize to anyone, ever.

"It's okay," I told him. "What were you supposed to think?"

We looked at each other.

2

"I'll look over the proposal," he said. "I'll get back to you soon."

I left his office and went back to my own desk. I hadn't written the fake proposal, but I wished I knew who did. Because it was true; Leon Fields was a cocksucking faggot, and he did eat shit, and I had always suspected that he liked it very much.

T hat evening I was telling my husband, Ed, about the little mystery at work when we heard the tapping for the first time. We were sitting at the dinner table, just finishing a meal of take-out Vietnamese.

Tap-tap.

We looked at each other.

"Did you hear that?"

"I think so."

Again: tap-tap. It came in twos or fours, never just one—tap-tap—and the sound had a drag on it, almost a scratching behind it, like claws on a wood floor.

First Ed stood up, then me. At first, the sound seemed to be coming from the kitchen. So we walked to the kitchen and bent down to listen under the base of the refrigerator and look under the stove, but then it seemed to be coming from the bathroom. In the bathroom we checked under the sink and behind the shower curtain, and then we determined it was coming from the bedroom. So we walked to the bedroom, and then to the living room, and then back to the kitchen again. After we toured the apartment we gave up. It was the pipes, we decided, something to do with the water flow or the heating system. Or maybe a mouse, running around and around the apartment inside the walls. Ed was revolted by the idea but I thought it was kind of cute, a little mouse with the spunk to make it up four stories and live on our few crumbs. We both forgot about the story I had been telling, and I never told Ed about the practical joke at work.

THE TAPPING went on for the rest of the winter. Not all the time, but for a few minutes every second or third night. Then at the end of the month I went to a conference on the West Coast for two days, and Ed noticed that he didn't hear it at all while I was gone. A few weeks later Ed went to a distant cousin's wedding up north for three days. The tapping went on all night, every night, while he was gone. I searched the apartment again, chasing the sound around and around. I examined the pipes, checked every faucet for drips, turned the heat on and off, and still the tapping continued. I cleaned the floors of any crumbs a rodent could eat, I even bought a carton of unpleasant little spring traps, and the sound was still there. I turned up the television, ran the dishwasher, spent hours on the phone with old, loud friends, and still I heard it.

Tap-tap.

I was starting to think this mouse wasn't so cute anymore.

T he noise wasn't so unusual, really; our building was close to a hundred years old and one expected that kind of noise. It had been built as an aspirin factory when the city still had an industrial base. After the industry moved out, one developer after another had tried to do something with the neighborhood, full of abandoned factories and warehouses like ours, but the schemes never took off. It was too far from the city, too desolate, too cold at night. As far as I was concerned it was better that the development hadn't gone as planned. Our building was still only half full. I liked the peace and quiet.

The first time we saw the loft I was absolutely sure it was the home for us. Ed needed a little convincing.

"Think of the quiet!" I told Ed. "No neighbors!"

Conduits were in place for lighting and plumbing but they had never been utilized. We would have to do major renovation. "Think of the possibilities!" I cried. "We can build it from scratch!"

Six white columns held up the place. Heat was provided by an industrial blower hung from the ceiling. "It has character," I told Ed. "It has a personality!"

He relented, and we got the place at half of what we would have paid elsewhere. We spent the extra money on renovation. Ed gave me free rein to do as I pleased. I was an architect and now I could be my own dream client. I designed every detail myself, from the off-white color of the walls to the porcelain faucets on the kitchen sink to the installation of the fireplace along the south wall, which cost a fortune, but was worth the money.

The neighborhood, though, was sometimes difficult. No supermarkets, no restaurants, a few small grocery stores that specialized in beer and cigarettes. The edge of the closest commercial district for shopping was ten blocks away, and the nearest residential area was on the other side of that. But we adjusted quickly. We had a car to take us wherever we wanted on nights and weekends, and during the week we usually took the train to work. Our other concern when we first moved in was the crime, but soon enough we found out there was none. It was too desolate even for criminals. I did, however, come to be scared of the stray dogs that patrolled the neighborhood. The dogs kept their distance and I kept mine but I always felt it was an uneasy truce. I didn't trust the animals to keep their side of the bargain. Walking home from the train I would spot one lurking in a doorway or on a street corner, eyeing me with suspicion. I was sure I would have preferred a mugger, who at least would only want my money—I didn't know what these dogs wanted when they looked at me with their bloodshot eyes.

That fall I found out when a German shepherd mix followed me home from the train station one night. I thought running would only provoke him, so I continued to walk at a regular pace, faking nonchalance. The German shepherd trailed behind at an equally steady pace, also faking nonchalance. At the entrance to my building, a steel door up two wide steps, I put my key in the lock and thought I was home free—the dog stayed on the street. And then in one great leap he jumped up the two steps and attacked. With his front paws, as strong as human hands, he pushed me against the wall, ignoring my horrified screams, licked me right on my mouth and tried to seduce me. When I finally convinced him I wasn't interested, he sat down by my feet, panting with a big smile. I spent a few minutes scratching behind his ears and then sneaked through the door.

I would have forgotten about him except that the next day he was waiting for me at the train station again, and the day after that. Walking home with him became a routine. He knew a few simple commands ("sit," "stay," "no") and I was convinced he had started off life as somebody's pet. I even went to a pet store and bought a bag of nutritionally balanced dog biscuits for him. On our walks home from the train I used the biscuits to teach him a few more commands—walk, lie down, stop-trying-to-fuck-me (which we abbreviated as *Stop*). I hoped that if I got him into more civilized condition I could find a home for him. I would have liked to take him in myself but Edward was allergic; dogs, cats, hamsters, strawberries, angora, and certain types of mushrooms were all hazardous materials, to be kept out of the apartment and handled with care.

But I was glad to have at least one friend in the neighborhood. And over the next few months it was my new friend, a nameless flea-ridden mutt, rather than Ed, who would be the first to see that I was not entirely myself.

NOT THAT Ed wasn't attentive, not that he didn't notice what was going on in my life. He just wasn't able to put the pieces together as quickly as the dog. Ed was my hero, my savior. Ed was the man who had imposed order on my chaotic life. When I was single, I'd eaten cereal for dinner and ice cream for lunch. I'd kept my tax records in a shopping bag in the closet. I'd spent Saturdays in a hungover fog, watching hours of old black-and-white movies. With Ed I spent Saturdays outdoors, doing the things I had always imagined I should do: flea markets, lunches, museums. He did our taxes, with itemized deductions, every January, and filed the records away in a real file cabinet. Here was a man who could finish any crossword puzzle, open any bottle, reach the top shelf at the grocery store without strain. Here was stability, here was something I could rely on, my rock, day in and day out. Someone who loved me, who would never leave me alone. You can't blame this sophisticated, civilized man for not having the same instincts as a wild dog.

W hat we think is impossible happens all the time. Like the time Ed let himself into the apartment and then lost his keys, somewhere in the house, and never found them again. Like the Halloween morning where I opened a cabinet of dishes, all stacked in perfect order, and the stack of plates on the highest shelf came toppling down, one by one, to bounce off my shoulders and shatter on the floor. Or when my friend Marlene picked up the phone to call her grandmother and someone was already on the line; one of her cousins, calling to tell her her grandmother had died that morning. We could devote our lives to making sense of the odd, the inexplicable, the coincidental, but most of us don't. And neither did I.

SOON AFTER the tapping began, Ed and I started to fight. We didn't fight all the time, we didn't change all at once. It was just a little bickering at first, I thought it was just a phase. I didn't know it was a part of a pattern, because I didn't know there was a pattern to see. I didn't know that it would escalate. If I had to pinpoint when the phase began—the phase that turned out not to be a phase at all but the start of a steady decline—I would say Valentine's Day of that year.

Our plan that Valentine's Day was to avoid the crowded restaurants and have a romantic night at home. I got off work first so I was in charge of dinner. Ed, due home at sevenish, was supposed to bring flowers and wine. By seven, I had cooked dinner—veal marsala and broccoli rabe—set the table, and had a store-bought chocolate soufflé in the oven. But then Ed called at 7:15 from the office and said he would be at least another hour or two. Some numbers had to be checked and rechecked and they couldn't wait until tomorrow. I watched the news on television, and then a few sitcoms. I ate a bag of pretzels watching a hospital drama. At eleven the news came on again. Not much had changed.

Well into the nighttime talk shows, Ed came strolling in the door with no flowers and no wine.

"Hi hon," he said, and walked across the loft to the sofa. He leaned in to give me a kiss. I pulled my head back. *How dare he*, I heard myself think.

"You're late," I said. *He's always late*, I thought. The tapping in the apartment was especially loud that night.

Tap-tap.

"I know, I'm sorry," he said with an exaggerated hound dog face. "Apology accepted?"

Tap-tap.

"No," I said. "Apology not fucking accepted."

"Oh honey, I—"

"It's VALENTINE'S DAY!" I yelled. "Where the fuck have you been?"

Tap-tap. Tap-tap.

"I called!" he yelled back. He walked into the bedroom to change into blue flannel pajamas and then yelled from there. "You knew I would be late!"

"You called four hours ago!"

Tap-tap. Tap-tap. Tap-tap. I was furious now. Nothing could make this okay.

"I'm sorry about dinner," he called, still in the bedroom. "I TOLD YOU I WAS SORRY!"

"You're always sorry!" I yelled back. "You and your FUCKING APOLOGIES!"

Tap-tap-tap-tap-tap—it reached a sort of crescendo and then stopped for the night.

Ed walked out of the bedroom and I walked in, slamming the door behind me. I lay in bed and in my mind reviewed every late night, every broken promise of my marriage. An hour later Ed came to bed and I pretended to be asleep.

THAT NIGHT I had an odd dream, which I remembered very clearly the next morning. A red ocean was rimmed with a shore of darker crimson sand. In the ocean a woman played in the waves. She was beautiful and had big dark eyes; her only flaw was her huge head of black hair, which was matted into dirty locks. I watched her from the shore. She walked out of the ocean and the red liquid rolled off her skin like mercury. Then we were lying next to each other on the sand. Her teeth were as pointy as fangs. I thought they were pretty.

"I like you," she said. She reached over and twirled a lock of my hair around her fingers. I blushed and looked down at the red sand.

"Can I stay with you?" she asked. With my index finger I spelled out YES in the crimson sand. Next to that she wrote her name: NAAMAH.

She put her arms around me and we hugged like sisters. I loved her so much, I wanted us to be together always.

I WAS sure I had seen that woman before. She came in and out of my mind often the next few days, like a few notes of a song you just couldn't reconnect to the whole. Especially her lips, I was sure I had seen them before. It was a few days later that the name came back to me. Ed and I were at the kitchen table with our morning coffee and toast, talking about his friends Alex and Sophia. We hadn't exactly made up from the Valentine's Day fight but we had let it go, silently decided that it had never happened. I was half listening to a story about Alex's promotion, half thinking about what to wear that day, when her name flew back to me, unannounced.

"Pansy!" I called out. "I *knew* I knew her."

*

PANSY HAD been an imaginary friend. I first thought of her when I was five or six. A mother substitute. I imagined her combing my hair, setting up for a tea party with me, tucking me into bed at night. My real mother had passed away when I was three—from a heart attack—and my father remarried very quickly, to a woman who had never wanted children. Noreen. Pansy wasn't another little girl, she was what I thought of as a grown-up, but she was really a teenager. She was modeled loosely on Tracy Berkowitz, a glamorous eighteen-year-old who lived down the block. But unlike Tracy, Pansy was wise and soothing and cared about me. I was not so lonely as to be deranged, to think that Pansy was real. There was no psychic break, no supernatural mischief. I was absolutely aware that I was real and Pansy was imaginary.

Until, one day, she wasn't. I was on my way home from school. The image that had loomed so large at six had, by the time I was nine, been relegated to a few minutes of attention before I went to sleep, where I imagined her kissing me good night. It was late spring, towards the end of the school year. The sun was bright and the hum of summer was already in the air, flies and crickets and the far-off sounds of Trans Ams and Camaros in town. I was walking home from school, down a block of neat white houses with patches of green lawn, each one almost identical to the next. I was walking slowly, not in a hurry to be home, or anywhere at all. The street was empty except for a woman at the end of the block, standing at the crossroads as if she was waiting for someone.

Without interest I noticed the woman on the corner. As I got closer she turned toward me and smiled. At first I thought she was Tracy Berkowitz. But no, I remembered, Tracy, unwed, had moved to the city months ago with her cop boyfriend. The move was a minor scandal on the block and there was no forgetting it.

The woman on the corner was looking right at me now. She had a mess of black hair and a pink pretty smile. I remember her skin, perfectly bisque with a soft translucent glow, like an airbrushed photo from a magazine.

It was Pansy.

My heart beat like a hummingbird in my chest. I went into a kind of panic, thoughts falling on top of each other with no order. It couldn't be her. But it was.

When I reached the corner she stepped in front of me, and I stopped. She bent down, leaning her hands on her thighs. The sun shone directly on her face, but she didn't blink or squint.

"Hi Amanda," she said. Her voice had a clear, sweet tone like a violin. All my fears dissipated when I heard that voice.

"Can you see me, Amanda?" she asked.

Just then a growling Firebird sped by the cross street, honking its horn. Instinctively I blinked and turned towards it, for a half second or less. When I turned back, she was gone.

I was old enough to know that this was impossible, what had just happened, and that only crazy people believed in impossible events. I buried the memory so deeply it didn't resurface until the dreams began.

Incidentally, my father and Noreen died while I was in my second year of college. They were scuba diving off the coast of Jamaica and got caught in a coral reef and drowned.

I TOLD Edward the whole story, about the woman I had seen as a child and the dreams I had had.

"So you saw a woman, when you were a girl, who looked like your imaginary friend, and last night you had a dream about her." Ed had a certain tone of voice, skeptical and a little condescending, which made him sound like a father whose daughter was late coming home from the prom. It wasn't one of his more attractive qualities.

"But who was that woman? Why did she know my name?"

"It was probably that Stacy woman."

"Tracy. But it wasn't Tracy. It was Pansy."

Ed sighed. "So it was Pansy," he said.

"Oh, forget it."

Edward put the paper down and reached across the table for my hand, which I reluctantly gave to him.

"Alex and Sophia said we could use their beach house the last weekend in September. You want to go?"

"Sure."

Alex and Sophia were old friends of Ed's. A few times a year they gave us the keys to their beach house outside the city.

"We both need to relax," Ed said.

There was no more talk of Pansy or nightmares for the rest of the morning. Maybe Ed was right, I thought: Pansy never had pointy teeth, and I never saw her naked. Naamah had bigger eyes. Pansy was shorter. But as the day went on and their faces came in and out of my mind I was sure the two women were one and the same. Naamah could have been Pansy, only a few years older. Pansy could have been Naamah, dressed and made up for a costume party.

And besides, I was pleased with the dream, in a way. To see Pansy again was like a visit from an old friend. I was irked with Edward but I quickly got over it. He was right, after all. I was stressed, and we did need to relax. Somehow that explained away the strange dreams— stress. As for what I had seen on the street that day when I was nine, I told myself Ed was right. It must have been Tracy after all.

WE COULD devote our lives to making sense of the odd, the inexplicable, the coincidental. But most of us don't, and I didn't either.

O n the whole, Ed and I were happy—with each other, with the loft, with our careers. He worked in the financial department of a large women's wear corporation, I was an architect at a small firm, and we did quite well. We didn't lack anything. We loved each other, and it wasn't yet clear that the phase of fighting we were in had become a trend.

I was twenty-eight when I met Edward. I felt lucky to have found him. He was a man you could trust, a big-boned healthy blond. No skeletons in his closet. A large family of not-too-observant Catholics. All of his obvious and possibly problematic neuroses (mostly descended from growing up as a middle child, I thought, never receiving enough attention) were channeled into a desire for success, which I found appealing. He didn't like sports or late night television, two big pluses. He had a good mind for details, a good memory, and a determination to follow through on his word: if he said he was going to call at three, he called at three. No surprises. That pretty much summed up Ed—no surprises. So when, after going out for two years, Ed said he wanted us to move in together, and if all went well, marry a year or two after that, I knew he meant what he said. I had been living in a little one bedroom downtown for three years. My apartment was cute and had its own charm, but it wasn't big enough for two. So I moved into Ed's place, a one bedroom in a modern apartment building near my office. Ed's place was a bit sterile, it had terrible cream-colored wall-to-wall carpeting and too much laminated furniture, but if all went well we planned to buy our own place within a few years.

Two years after we'd moved in together, we got married in a small private ceremony at city hall. It was either that or a huge blowout, which we both thought was a little tacky—Edward had five brothers and sisters and dozens of cousins, aunts, uncles, nieces and nephews, plus there were our friends, business associates, on and on. Rather than inviting them all, we invited no one. We went to city hall in the morning, got married, and went out to lunch at our favorite dim sum house with some friends afterwards. Soon after that we started looking for a home to buy, and found the loft.

OF COURSE, our life together wasn't always perfect. All couples argue and we were no different. There were a few things about Ed, small things, that drove me crazy. For instance he was almost compulsively neat—a scrap of paper on the coffee table for longer than a day or two would upset him. He was also given to a rigidity that could be slightly repulsive, like an elderly English bachelor—if there was no thin-sliced white bread for toast in the morning he could be thrown into a mood for hours. And he didn't take any deviation from a plan well—he wasn't one for getting lost in the countryside, or for long, aimless walks around the city. And the fact that when Ed chewed gum he would swallow it instead of spitting it out . . . for some indefinable reason that revolted me no end. And the toast, and the toothpaste cap that absolutely must be replaced immediately, and the shirts that had to be folded just so, and all the other little routines that had to be followed every day. Over six years, though, I had become accustomed to a certain amount of irritation, as I'm sure all spouses do, and these were small arguments and disappointments that didn't interrupt the steady flow of our marriage. When we started to argue a bit more than usual, when Ed's habits and rituals began to irritate me a bit more often, I was sure that it would pass.

SHE WAS subtle at first. It wasn't like everything went wrong all at once. Suppose you're looking at a bottle of whiskey. And one part of you says, *Gee, I'd really like a sip of that whiskey.* Then another part pipes in and says, *Well, you shouldn't, you have to drive home, and you know whiskey's very fattening.* And then a third part says, *Just drink it.* This mental voice is new, it's a sound you're not accustomed to hearing in your own head, but it's not that different either, it's done a good job of imitating your own silent voice and you like what it's saying. Come on. Don't stop. Don't think. It'll be fun. Just drink it. Now.

You wouldn't guess that the third part wasn't you. You'd probably just drink the whiskey.

IN MARCH I started smoking again, which gave us more to fight about. I had quit when I first moved in with Ed. He said he was allergic to smoke. I thought he just never learned to appreciate the sharp bitter smell, like a smouldering fireplace, of a burning cigarette. But I knew it was for the best, and privately I was a little ashamed of myself for violating my body day in and day out. So I quit. Living in the new apartment helped. No ashtrays. No Formica kitchen table where I would sit and talk on the phone, cigarette in hand. A new apartment, a new life, new habits. I had a few sessions with an acupuncturist and it wasn't too hard, just sad, like an old friend moving out of town.

I started smoking again on a gray, drizzling Monday. I was on my lunch hour, eating a sandwich at a little coffee shop near my office. I had a newspaper open in front of me but I wasn't reading. Instead, I eavesdropped on the couple next to me. She was about my age, maybe a little younger, and had blonde hair pulled back into a knot. He was much older and looked out of place, more accustomed to the kind of restaurant that had a wine list and a maître d'. They talked about a trip to the Caribbean. When I stood up to leave my eyes caught hers. She gave me a sly little smile, almost a wink, and then lit a cigarette. The smoke rolled over the few inches to my table, and when the smell hit me I became weak. I watched the woman, her attention turned back to her partner, inhale deeply and then exhale, sending more of the woodsy smoke in my direction. She was clearly a longtime smoker; the cigarette fit into her hand, as natural and practical as a sixth digit. Like a starving woman looking at a steak, I wanted that cigarette. I imagined how easy it would be: *Excuse me, do you have another smoke? I'm sorry, can I bother you for a cigarette? Can I bum one of those? Do you have an extra? Give me one. Give it to me.*

I left the cafe, planning to distract myself with the change in scenery. But outside, where the rain came down in a thin, steady drizzle, it seemed every person I passed had a cigarette in their hand, either lighting one or smoking one or putting one out. And the smokers looked so happy, so healthy, so satisfied with their smoking. How is it, I asked myself, that all this time I've thought smoking was dirty and toxic? Look at these people—they're glowing! The cigarette mottoes ran through my head. A thin woman in a black trenchcoat inhaled deeply from a long Waverly—The Smoker's Choice. A fit, middle-aged man in a three-piece suit lit a Texas straight—The Tasteful Smoke. I tried the breathing exercises the acupuncturist had taught me but with each inhalation I brought in the crisp taste of burning tobacco. I walked back to the cobblestone block where my office was, hoping for relief. It was even worse. In each doorway a person lingered with a cigarette, embers glowing in each direction.

Kensington—The Mild Cigarette. Fairfax—The Refreshing Taste. Embassy Means Smoking Enjoyment. Lowes Means More Smoking Pleasure. I was almost at the office, and I knew that once inside the purified air I would be fine—but I had one more hurdle to jump. In the doorway of the building was a small, pale woman with long black hair in a tight black dress. She was smoking a Midwood Medium, my favorite. The Satisfying Smoke.

I stood in front of the woman with the black hair. It would be so easy to ask—but no, I wouldn't. I opened my mouth to say *Excuse me*, so I could press my way into the safety of my office. But when I opened my mouth and set my lips and tongue into motion, I found they were not my own at all. In my mind I made the *x* of *excuse me* at the top of my throat, but the tip of my tongue instead reached to the bony part of my upper palate to say, "Do you have another smoke?"

"Sure," said the woman with a smile. She reached into her purse for the pack and a book of matches, shook out a cigarette and held it out to me.

And so I started smoking again. I tried to convince myself with a circle of assumptions; I had asked for a cigarette, so I must have wanted a cigarette. Lack of willpower. My subconscious desires had overridden my superego. I circled around and around for a week before I just accepted the fact I was smoking again, and I would have to live with it or go through another long withdrawal. And Edward would have to live with it, too.

It took him a while to see that. When he first found a pack of cigarettes in my purse he was pure disappointment. It was my health, he said, he was so worried about my health. When that didn't work, it was the allergies, which I had long ago learned didn't need quite as much coddling as Ed led one to believe. His arguments fell on deaf ears. I was enjoying smoking again. I felt more like myself. I thought I might keep smoking for the rest of my life. Next his campaign picked up a little cruelty; I smelled bad, my teeth were turning yellow, smoking was filthy, low class. These weren't attributes that particularly bothered me, and I noticed they didn't bother most of the men I met, either. He pleaded, he yelled, finally, he gave up.

I felt wonderful, like my old friend was back in town. Sort of like seeing Pansy again, after all those years.

There was the tapping, and the fighting, and the smoking, and the dreams, and I never would have thought to link them if it hadn't been for a mistake, or what seemed like a mistake at the time. I had ordered a book from a small publisher out of state—*Design Issues Past and Present*—that I was hoping would inspire me a bit with a project at work. I came home to the loft one rainy April night pleased to find a package waiting by the door. But when I got upstairs and opened the box I saw they had sent the wrong book—*Demon Possession Past and Present*—instead. A disappointment, but nothing to cry about. I put the book on the coffee table, forgot about it, and went about making dinner.

After dinner was made I sat on the sofa. Ed was late again. Out of boredom I picked up the accidental book, *Demon Possession Past and Present*.

On the first page there was a little quiz:

Are YOU Possessed by a Demon?

1. I hear strange noises in my home, especially at night, which family members tell me only occur when I am present.

27

2. I have new activities and pastimes that seem "out of character," and I do things that I did not intend and do not understand.

3. I'm short- and ill-tempered with my friends and loved ones.

4. I can understand languages I've never studied, and have the ability to know things I couldn't know through ordinary means.

5. I have blackouts not caused by drugs, alcohol, or a preexisting health condition.

6. I have unusual new thoughts, or hear voices in my head.

7. I've had visions or dreams of personalities who may be demons.

8. A psychic, minister, or other spiritualist has told me I'm possessed.

9. I have urges to hurt or kill animals and other people.

10. I have hurt or killed animals or people.

On the next page was an analysis of the quiz results. I had scored a four out of ten; there was the noise in our apartment, I had started smoking again, I had been fighting with Ed, and I had been having strange dreams.

0–3: You are probably not possessed. See a doctor or mental health professional for an evaluation.

3–6: You may be haunted, or in the early stages of possession. Do not be alarmed. Seek a spiritual counselor for assistance.

6–10: You are possessed. Consult with your spiritual counselor immediately. You may be a threat to the safety of yourself and your family.

Possession usually begins with a preliminary stage called "obsession"—the obsession of the demon with the victim. In this stage the victim is still alone in his body but all five senses, and in addition the memory and mind, can be manipulated and disturbed by the Entity. The victim may feel lust, envy, greed, or urges towards any of the sins with stronger force than ever before. It is common for the victim to hear the demon in the form of rapping, tapping, or scratching that seems to follow them around; also common is for the victim to have their dreams infiltrated by the Possessing Entity.

I put the book down and picked up a fat biography of Frank Lloyd Wright I had been meaning to read for months. But just a few pages in, as quiet as a mouse and loud as a gunshot, there it was again.

Tap-tap.

That same annoying noise. But it was clearer tonight.

Now that I listened to it carefully I was sure it wasn't the pipes at all. And it was far too loud for a mouse.

Tap-tap. Tap-tap.

I was beginning to get uneasy. I stood up and walked around the apartment. Nothing. It was just like before; the sound was always close, but never exactly where I was looking. If I was in the kitchen, it was in the bedroom. If I went to the bedroom, it seemed to be coming from the bathroom. I gave up and went back to the sofa. I picked up a magazine from the coffee table. Miniskirts were coming back into style.

Tap-tap.

I was more and more uneasy. It had never been this loud before. The rain outside blew against the windows and I tried to tell myself the sound was just the rain, tapping on the glass. Or the pipes. Or a faucet.

Tap-tap. Tap-tap.

Alone in the quiet apartment, I now heard that it wasn't a tapping at all. More like a pitter-patter. It continued with a steady tattoo around and around the apartment. It sounded like footsteps, scratching steps like a dog or a cat running quickly over a wood floor, claws scraping on the wood.

Pitter-patter, pitter-patter.

Of course it wasn't footsteps. No one lived above us and there was obviously no one in the apartment with me. The sound got louder, closer. It couldn't be footsteps. As much as it sounded like footsteps there was no way, it was absolutely impossible, I shouldn't even let it cross my mind that the sound could be footsteps. I stared at the magazine. Slingbacks were the shoes to wear with the new miniskirts.

Pitter-patter, pitter-patter.

The sound that wasn't footsteps came closer. It circled around and around the sofa. I stopped pretending to read the magazine. It was in front of me, pacing back and forth in front of the sofa.

Pitter-patter, pitter-patter.

It stopped right in front of me. I couldn't move. I was sure I was hyperventilating. Just then I heard a noise to my left and I screamed.

Ed. Just Ed, coming home.

I SAW her again in a dream that night. I was sitting on the sofa, listening to the tap-tapping, like I had been that evening. I looked down at the floor and I saw a pair of feet. Small, perfect white feet that seemed to materialize from thin air.

I looked up. Above me I saw a bright, black eye. She was standing right in front of me, and yet it was as if I was looking through a keyhole. I couldn't see her all at once. I saw a pert white nose, and then in a separate view the pink lips wrapped around pointed white teeth. If I looked down at her small white foot I lost sight of everything above the knee. If I looked at her hand all I saw was a hand, with long unpolished nails.

"Don't fight, Amanda," she said with her pink lips.

The room went black. I was falling, slipping down out of myself into a warm damp blackness. She took me to the crimson beach. We lay on the sand and watched the fish jump in and out of the ruby sea. Here I could see her clearly, as a whole.

"I choose you," she said.

"You'll never leave?" I asked.

"Never," she said. "Nothing can get me out."

She put her arms around me and pulled me tight against her. Our ribs crushed together and our hipbones slammed and she pulled me tighter until I couldn't breathe, I was choking, and my spine met hers, vertebrae against vertebrae.

I didn't bother to read the rest of *Demon Possession Past and Present* right then. But I did put it on the bookshelf instead of returning it like I had planned. It was too late, I reasoned, for the other book to be useful now anyway—the project was due in a few days, and it would never get here on time. Besides, maybe someday it would be good for a laugh.

AND ANOTHER funny little thing I noticed. After that night, that dream, I never heard the tapping in the apartment again, and neither did Ed.

ON SATURDAY morning we decided to drive downtown to run a few errands. Ed had run out of his allergy pills. He didn't need them every day, but they were important to have on hand in case he came across an errant cat or a renegade strawberry. I needed a bottle of hair conditioner and had also been thinking about a new toothbrush. We had been meaning to start checking prices on dishwashers—the old one left a thin layer of grime inside the coffee cups. And there was a Tibetan restaurant nearby where we liked to get lunch. In the car we bickered over which drugstore to go to. Like all couples we had developed our own language, a shorthand of associations and memories.

"Are we going to the Italian?"

"Too expensive. Want to go to the crazy lady place?"

"They don't have my conditioner there. How about the place with the socks?"

"I hate that place. How about the big place?"

"Which big place?"

"The new one, near the crappy French restaurant."

"Which crappy French restaurant?"

"The one where we went with Marlene, and she got the soup with the—"

"OH! Right, right, right. Near the Tibetan place."

"Right."

"Sure, let's go there."

In the big drugstore, a quarter of a city block, Ed waited on line to fill his prescription while I found my toothbrush and then my conditioner. With time to kill, I browsed the cosmetics section. I was looking at a cute red lipstick when Ed found me. He had his pills. We paid and left to go to the Tibetan restaurant for lunch.

On our way out of the drugstore we heard a rapid, high-pitched beep.

"Step back." A teenage security guard ordered us back through the alarm. Ed and I rolled our eyes at each other and stepped back into the store. After a nod from the security guard we stepped back out.

Beep-beep-beep.

The guard waved his hand for us to step back in. We stepped back in.

"Open your bags, please."

We rolled our eyes at each other again. Ed opened his bag, which held the pills, toothbrush, and conditioner, and fumbled in his pocket for the receipt. The guard nodded approval and then turned his attention to my purse. I held it open with an exaggerated sigh. He peered down into the bag and poked a hand in to rummage through the contents: wallet, keys, scraps of paper, change purse. After a quick minute he pulled his hand out, a black tube of lipstick held between his thumb and forefinger. It was sealed in clear plastic and had a wide white alarm strip wrapped around it.

"You have a receipt for this?"

I stared at him, shocked. "That's not mine."

"I'm going to ask you to come with me, ma'am." He put his hand on my arm to lead me toward the back of the store. I pulled my arm free.

"Get your fucking hands off me!"

The guard looked at Ed and me. "Do you want to tell me how this lipstick got in your purse?"

"I have no idea," I told him truthfully. "It must have fallen in. I was looking at it, but then I put it back. Seriously, I have no idea. Look—" I opened my wallet, which held a few hundred in twenties. "Do you think I would steal a four-dollar lipstick?"

"It's in your purse," he said.

"Listen," said Ed. "We'll pay for it. How's that?"

"But I don't even want it!" I protested.

Ed ignored me and looked at the guard, a come-on-we're-all-men-here look. "I'll pay for it."

After a dramatic pause the security guard nodded. He escorted us back to the cashier, where Ed paid for the lipstick, and then we left.

Outside the store we looked at each other in astonishment, shaking our heads as we walked towards the Tibetan restaurant. I lit a cigarette and for once Ed didn't scowl.

"I can't believe it," I said. I really couldn't. "I haven't stolen anything since seventh grade." When I was twelve and my stepmother said I was too young for makeup I went on a shoplifting spree, ending when I was caught red-handed with a contraband eyeliner.

"Maybe he put it there," said Ed. "Thought you wouldn't put up a fuss."

"Why would he want to do that?"

We were silent for a moment, contemplating the possible motivations of a rogue security guard.

Ed shrugged. "It must have fallen, like you said."

"Yeah. I guess when I put it back in the dispenser it fell back out."

"It must have."

"Must have."

"Yeah. It must have."

First Ed burst out laughing, then me. Almost arrested in the drugstore, over a four-dollar lipstick I hadn't even wanted! We told the story again and again to friends and coworkers, and even to Ed's mother, over the phone. It was too funny. Hysterical. And even funnier was that at the end I was glad to have the lipstick; it was a dark, brick red that I never would have bought, far from my usual neutral, pinkish brown, but for the rest of that summer and fall I wore the red lipstick almost every day and when it ran out, in mid-November, I went back to the same drugstore and stole another tube.

L eaving work a few days later I walked by a hole-in-the-wall bar between my office and the train. I had walked by it a hundred times before without a second thought. Suddenly I wanted a drink. *One drink*, I thought. *Just one.* It had been years since I stopped in to a bar, alone, for a drink. I stood in front of the door. It looked filthy inside. *One drink*, I thought. *Just one quick drink.*

An hour later I was on my third tequila, sitting at the bar with a man whose name I had instantly forgotten when he introduced himself to me. He was about my age, with short, scruffy black hair and an appealing, slightly wrinkled face. His arms were wrapped in tattoos; Japanese goldfish with bulging eyes and a mermaid with a sweet face and waves and waves of water in between. This was the kind of man I liked in my early twenties, before I met Ed.

"How about four," the bartender said. I nodded. The man I was sitting with smiled. He had a once-in-a-lifetime smile. The bartender gave us two more drinks.

I looked around the room. Mostly men, mostly tattooed like my drinking companion. A band was setting up or breaking down in one corner of the room.

"You can drink," the man said.

"I can," I answered, but I didn't feel drunk at all. Just happy to be out, having fun.

I GOT home late and Ed, naturally, was worried and angry in equal parts. I didn't bother to apologize, or even make up a very convincing lie.

"Worked late, hon."

Edward sulked, sitting on the sofa in boxer shorts and an undershirt. "I was worried. You could have called."

I ignored him and went to the bedroom to undress. In a red kimono I walked back to the bathroom and drew myself a bath, ignoring Edward again when I walked through the living room.

Let him worry, I told myself. Let him see what it's like, sitting alone, watching the clock, waiting for your spouse to come home. I lay down in the hot water and poured in half a bottle of lily-of-the-valley bubble bath, a birthday gift from Ed I had been saving for a special occasion. My spine and neck relaxed in the soft hot water. I knew we would have a fight after I got out of the bathtub. Ed would ask what my problem was and I would say I didn't have a problem and he would say I was sure acting like I had a problem. Then I would say I guess the problem is that you think one member of the household can come and go as he pleases while the other has to account for every minute of her time. And he would say where the hell were you tonight. And I would say at the office, like

I said. Call and check if you want. And he would look at the phone on its little desk by the bookcases, sitting there like a slug, and then look back at me. Forget it, he would say. Fine, I would say. Fine, he would say. We would go to bed chilly and wouldn't warm up again until the next morning, or the next evening over dinner.

TWO WEEKS later. Another night at home. Another take-out dinner, shared late. We had made up from the last blowout but there was still a chill between us, a polite caution that replaced affection. After dinner we sat on the sofa together and disappeared into our separate worlds. A documentary about World War II was on television. Summer had come on quickly and it was so hot in the loft that Ed, who dressed immaculately even at home, left his usual summer cotton pajamas in the dresser and wore just a clean pair of white-and-blue-striped boxer shorts and a white undershirt. I had on a thin camisole and another pair of his clean white-and-blue-striped boxers. Edward flipped through a magazine. I flipped through a book on midcentury furniture design.

I lit a cigarette. Edward gently rolled his eyes. We had made an agreement that I would keep smoking in the loft to a minimum, a concession to Ed's tragic allergies. I ignored him. I smoked and looked at my book, half listening to the television. The cigarette was in its usual place between the first and second fingers of my right hand.

I thought, *What if I stuck Edward with this cigarette?*

Everyone has thoughts like this from time to time: What if I burned my husband? What if I pushed him off this cliff? What if I jumped off this roof? The thought came into my head and then disappeared just as quickly. I lifted the cigarette to my lips for a last drag. Then, in my mind, I took it down to stub it out in the little white custard cup I used as an ashtray. Very nice, French, we had gotten a set of six as a wedding present, I don't remember from whom. I do know that I never before or after made a custard. In my mind my hand moved towards the table and snuffed out the cigarette in the little white cup. My fingers, with a chipped brown manicure, were at my lips, the brown filter suspended between the first and second fingers of my right hand. I took the last drag and then released my lips. I assumed my hand would move down to the table and put out the cigarette.

It didn't. Instead my hand made a quick turn to the right and stabbed the burning cigarette into Edward's leg, an inch above his left knee.

He screamed. I screamed. I ran into the kitchen for ice and Edward kept screaming. He jumped up from the sofa screaming bloody murder.

"Shit! Fuck! What the fuck did you do that for? What the hell is wrong with you?"

I was speechless. Edward sat back down, still cursing. I sat next to him and held a bag of frozen peas over the burn. The screaming tapered off into a muttering, and then silence. He closed his eyes and leaned back.

"What happened?" he asked, after a few minutes. He wasn't really angry. Just shocked.

"I don't know," I told him. "I didn't mean to."

"Of course you didn't mean to," he said. "I know that."

"I don't know what happened. My arm just moved. I didn't mean to. How're you feeling?"

"Terrible," he answered. "It hurts like hell."

"I'm sorry."

"Don't be sorry." He reached over and ruffled the hair on top of my head. "It was an accident."

"I love you," I said.

"I love you too," he answered.

"I don't know what happened. It's like it moved by itself."

"Maybe it's tendinitis. Julian's wife had it in her shoulder and she couldn't even hold her arm up. It used to just flop all over the place."

"I don't think so," I told him. "My shoulder feels fine."

"You twitched," said Edward. "A spasm."

I knew it wasn't tendinitis. My arm hadn't flopped. It hadn't slipped, it hadn't twitched, it hadn't fallen. It had moved by itself. It had moved with a controlled movement away from the ashtray and towards Edward's leg.

Edward didn't say anything, and neither did I. There was nothing to say.

THE DAY after I burned Edward, I took *Demon Possession Past and Present* down from the bookshelf and took the little quiz again. Not that I took it seriously. Not that I for a moment believed anything so ridiculous as that a demon or devil was influencing my life.

Are YOU Possessed by a Demon?

1. I hear strange noises in my home, especially at night, which family members tell me only occur when I am present.

2. I have new activities and pastimes that seem "out of character," and I do things that I did not intend and do not understand.

3. I'm short- and ill-tempered with my friends and loved ones.

4. I can understand languages I've never studied, and have the ability to know things I couldn't know through ordinary means.

5. I have blackouts not caused by drugs, alcohol, or a preexisting health condition.

6. I have unusual new thoughts, or hear voices in my head.

7. I've had visions or dreams of personalities who may be demons.

8. A psychic, minister, or other spiritualist has told me I'm possessed.

9. I have urges to hurt or kill animals and other people.

10. I have hurt or killed animals or people.

This time I scored a five.

0–3: You are probably not possessed. See a doctor or mental health professional for an evaluation.

3–6: You may be haunted, or in the early stages of possession. Do not be alarmed. Seek a spiritual counselor for assistance.

6–10: You are possessed. Consult with your spiritual counselor immediately. You may be a threat to the safety of yourself and your family.

I read a bit more:

Some other signs of possession include a change in appearance and changes in personality that may be so subtle even those close to the victim may not be able to pinpoint the difference. Generally speaking, an over-all increase in aggressive behavior is to be expected. However, until the very late stages of possession, the victim continues with his daily life largely intact . . . A sudden psychic ability is almost always present, and is in fact one of the first definite signs to look for when in doubt. Another common characteristic is the insatiable need to be desired by members of the opposite sex.

45

*

LEAVING MY hairdresser's the next afternoon, I ran into a woman I knew. Bernadette Schwartz worked at Ed's company. She had been a model when she was younger and she still looked like one, tall and stunning with perfect long chestnut hair. I knew her a little, through company Christmas parties, and we stopped to say hello. She gave me a good hard look.

"What is it?" she asked. She peered at me with huge brown eyes, now ugly and accusatory.

"What's what?"

"You. Did you get work done?"

"Work?"

"An eye lift or something. Or maybe your teeth. You look different."

"Huh." I looked at myself in a mirror across from us. A mirror behind us was reflected into the first and I saw a funhouse, an infinite number of mirrors, each with a picture of me. I did look different; as if I had had a good night's sleep, or even a year's worth of good nights. My skin was bright and my eyes shiny. My whole face was plumped up, all the little lines of thirty-four smooth as satin.

"I know," said Bernadette, "you're *pregnant*!"

I rubbed my eyes and shook my head and then looked back at the mirror. My own true face, a little haggard, now looked back at me. Bernadette frowned.

"New haircut?" she ventured, less sure of herself now.

46

"Just a trim," I said. "Must be the weather. This humidity, it's always good for my skin."

WHEN I got out of the train station that evening the German shepherd was waiting as usual, sitting quietly as I'd trained him to do. The routine was he wouldn't stand up to give me a kiss (the one untoward act I allowed him) until I had given him his first biscuit. I went to the corner where he sat waiting. Usually his tail would be wagging by now and there would be a big drooling smile on his face. But he sat, moping, as if I hadn't shown up at all. He looked away from me and then right through me. I took a biscuit, shaped like a cartoon bone, out of my purse and held it out to him.

He sniffed at the biscuit and looked up at me with his big watery eyes, but he didn't take it. Instead he stiffened his back and shoulders and snarled at me, baring a row of yellow plaque-covered teeth. I dropped the biscuit and ran home.

When Ed got home I told him what had happened.

"Well," he said, "I told you not to mess around with strays."

Ed didn't believe that just because something was alive, that meant you had to love it.

I didn't obsess about the incident with the cigarette. I didn't make much of the book. Ed had forgotten easily enough. So I'd twitched. I'd slipped. I'd spasmed. It was summer and with the sun so bright it was hard to think about demons, hard to think about pain.

But two weeks later, at the Fitzgerald house, I had a little twitch again.

I had decided to become an architect when I was twenty. I had moved to the city when I was eighteen, to go to college, and I started with a major in art. I was in love—with my school, with the city, with the snow. I had come from a southern suburb where every star was brightly visible at night and the thermometer never dropped below fifty. I had spent eighteen years in continual boredom. Then when I was twenty my father and Noreen had died and left me nothing. Everything that could have and should have been mine had been eaten up by Noreen's fur coats and facial treatments. I went through the labyrinthine process of applying for financial aid and as part of the deal, got a job in the Department of Architecture office. One thing I noticed about the architects was that they dressed a hell of a lot better than the art professors. And they drove better cars. And they seemed a lot more likely to have spouses and even children, too. So I switched to the architecture program. After graduation I worked for one of my professors for a year, then moved to a big firm for a few years where I never even met three of the four partners, and then on to Fields & Carmine, where I had been for the past three years.

The Fitzgerald house was my largest project to date. I had high hopes; if all went according to plan I had a chance at an A.I.A. award and maybe a spread in *Design Monthly*, plus recommendations from the Fitzgeralds and their rich friends. If all went well, then the larger plan, to open my own firm, could be accelerated by years.

The job reminded me of Michelangelo's line about sculpting a block of stone; he chipped away everything that wasn't *David*. The Fitzgeralds, a nice millionaire couple my own age, had bought an old Victorian mansion in a run-down part of town. Even with an unlimited budget they couldn't find the space they wanted anywhere else. The huge Victorian had been converted first into three apartments, and then divided up further into a twelve-unit rooming house. You could get lost for hours imagining who had roomed there, but never mind. The task at hand was to turn the rooming house back into a mansion. I was working with a team of designers, decorators, plumbers, electricians, painters, air-conditioning specialists, woodworkers, and carpenters, and we would chip away all the divisions, additions, and ornament that weren't the Fitzgeralds' house.

On a Wednesday morning I stopped by on my way to the office to see how the work was coming along. No one else was there. It was only eight-thirty and the workers wouldn't come in until nine or ten. The house was chilly inside. Only a few streaks of light filtered in through the shuttered windows. It was quiet and smelled like dust and plaster. I walked through the first floor. Half the rooming house partitions were torn down. They hadn't started to clean up yet and rubble was piled around empty door frames and steel beams. Eventually all the walls would come down and the first floor would be like a loft within the house—kitchen, dining room, living room, all in one open space.

I climbed the stairs, avoiding the thick dust on the mahogany bannisters. The house was filthy. My footsteps echoed off the endless yards of white drywall. Upstairs we would rebuild the original bedrooms, four of them, for a nice balance of openness and privacy. It would be great when they had kids. For now, each bedroom was still split into two lonely cubicles. A few odds and ends from the house's previous incarnations were still lying around: a yo-yo with a broken string sat in one corner; a stained brown tie hung over a hook on the wall; one worn black shoe lingered in a hallway.

Everything looked fine. I walked down to the first floor and was about to leave when I saw something I hadn't noticed before. A red glass doorknob on the living-room door.

I could swear it hadn't been there earlier. In fact, I could swear I had never seen one like it. I had noticed a few pretty, clear cut glass doorknobs around the house, and even one that was violet. Nothing special. But a smooth ruby red glass doorknob, without a scratch or a chip—I was sure I had never seen one like it before. In this sad white house here was a perfect round of red.

I want it, I thought. I took out the small tool kit I carried in my purse, released the tiny screws from the steel base, turned it out of its hole, and had the doorknob off in two minutes. I stuck it in my purse and left.

I didn't give it another thought until half an hour later. I was waiting for a train to take me to the office when I realized with horror that I had stolen a piece of my clients' house. What if I was found out? What if the Fitzgeralds noticed their doorknob missing? My career shot to hell over a doorknob. I thought about throwing it out. I knew I should bring it back.

But I did neither. I wanted it, and I kept it.

At home I installed my beautiful new ruby on the bathroom door. Ed came home later that evening, after I was in bed, and didn't see the new doorknob until the next morning. I told him I picked it up at a design show-room. We stood in front of the bathroom door, still in our underwear. He scrunched his brow.

"I don't know," he said. "Do you think it goes?"

"Yes," I said. "It goes perfectly."

He frowned. "It's *red*."

"I know. That's what I like about it."

"It's bright. Don't you think it's kind of bright?"

"We're keeping it," I said. Ed looked at me, a question written on his face. "We're keeping it," I said again, and went to the bedroom to dress.

I WAS on my way to work that morning when a black limousine, the size of two sedans, took a corner too close to the curb and splashed me with water from the gutter. Without thinking I walked up to the dark tinted driver's window of the car, now stopped behind a line of traffic, and tapped on the cold glass. No answer. I tapped again, hard enough this time to rattle the glass in its frame. A driver in a suit and plastic-brimmed cap rolled down the window. He had pink skin and copper hair pulled into a narrow ponytail, with a copper mustache to top it all off. He scowled at me.

"Yeah?"

"You should apologize," I said.

"What the fuck?" spat out the moustache.

"You should," I repeated, "apologize. Now." I leaned my face into the window and breathed in the leathery smell of the clean car. The driver had two choices now; apologize or push me out. He made a face and cursed under his breath.

"I'm sorry," he finally spat out, dripping with sarcasm.

"I'm sincerely fucking sorry. Now get out of the car."

I stood back up, and he rolled the window closed. As the glass came up I saw my reflection. Distorted in the glass my hair looked longer and darker, my skin smoother, and my lips as red as the ruby doorknob.

WE WERE on the crimson sand by the blood red sea. Her name was still spelled out on the sand.

"You're mine," she said. She licked my cheek with a tongue as stiff and wet as a snake.

I looked into her eyes. "You'll never leave?"

"Never." She wrapped her arms tighter around me. "Never never never."

"Why me?" I asked.

She didn't answer. Instead she smiled and licked my nose in a thin straight line from bottom to top.

When I woke up I could still feel the damp trace of her tongue on my face.

ED AND I had another fight the next morning. Lately I hadn't been as neat and orderly around the house as usual, which drove him up the wall.

"Amanda, please," he said. He was looking at a pile of yesterday's clothes, left on the bedroom floor. He was standing in the middle of the bedroom in socks, underwear, and a pale blue oxford shirt, scowling at the clothes.

Usually I would have picked them up and put them in the hamper where, after all, they belonged. This morning, though, I didn't want to put the clothes away. No reason. I just didn't want to.

"Yes?" I said to Edward. I was still in bed—or rather back in bed, having woken up, gotten a cup of coffee, a cigarette, and an ashtray, and returned. So I would be a little late to work. Big deal.

"Amanda, these clothes!" He was clearly irritated now, shifting his weight from one foot to another, torn between falling a minute or two behind schedule and dealing with the vital situation at hand.

"What about them?"

Ed scrunched his face and looked at me for a long anxious moment. He looked ridiculous, and it was hard to hold back a giggle.

"Oh, FORGET IT!" he said, and picked up the clothes himself. Not wanting to delay his schedule any further, he let the matter drop. I was sure it would be picked back up again when he came home that evening.

T he connections slowly began to knit themselves together. One bright summer morning I was sitting at a conference table looking over plans for Linda Marcello's cottage for the umpteenth time. Linda Marcello was a longtime Fields & Carmine client. We were renovating her summer cottage upstate. Linda was difficult; she wanted light in the shade, she wanted a dark brown room to feel "airy," she wanted a terrace with no visible means of support. I was daydreaming about being outdoors, at the park or maybe the beach. My hand, moving to point out a walk-in closet, brushed against hers. When our skin touched I saw Linda in her cottage, in the brown room that wasn't airy at all, sitting on the brown velvet sofa. I saw it as clearly as a movie rolling before my eyes. She sat on the sofa doing nothing, waiting for her husband to come home. He was due home hours ago. The boredom was excruciating. She looked around the room. What had she been thinking, with the brown? It could drive a person crazy, this room. She would have liked to go out but he wouldn't be happy if he came home and she wasn't there. Then the movie stopped and a new film started; I saw Linda again, ten years younger, in a cozy, cluttered white-walled apartment with two other young women. They were laughing and drinking wine—I couldn't make out all the words, but it was the kind of bonding/complaining conversation that young women have when they talk about men. They had all wanted to marry rich. Linda had.

The entire episode had taken only a second. Linda had no idea. Now I knew just the right thing to say.

"Did you see the paper today?" I asked. Linda shook her head. "The Marsha Merkon case finally closed. You know, the model, I mean former model, who was married to the head of Bluechip Securities."

"Oh really?" Linda turned around and looked at me with great interest—the first time, I think, she ever looked at me at all. This was one of those big divorce cases with enough money and lurid accusations involved to make tabloid headlines on slow news days. I knew that Linda would have been following the case.

"Yep. She got twenty million. And you know she's not even fifty. Now she's got twenty million dollars and her whole life ahead of her. You know what she said?"

"What?" Linda asked.

"That she would have divorced him no matter what, even if she hadn't gotten anything. That she felt younger than she had in ten years."

"Huh," she said. She was smiling now, her eyes almost as bright as they had been back in that shabby little apartment with her girlfriends. "You know I met her a few times, at parties. She wasn't at all like the papers made her out to be. She was a very nice woman. In fact, we talked about having lunch sometime."

"Well, this is probably a good time to call her," I said. "You can take her out to celebrate."

"Or she can take me out, with her twenty million," Linda said, laughing.

The next evening, paying for two steaks, touching the butcher's hand, I saw a clean, warm house where he lived with his wife and two young sons. The man who sold me my morning coffee, I saw a few days later, hated me. He hated all of us, going to our easy jobs in cushy offices while he got up at three in the morning to serve us our precious fucking coffee.

This new vision waxed and waned over the rest of the summer, and I was never sure what to make of it. More often than not, I ignored the snapshots that burst to life before my closed eyes, I dismissed them as fantasy—I had always daydreamed a lot.

I didn't tell Ed about it. He was a devout agnostic, and believed anything that smacked of metaphysics or the supernatural was mumbo jumbo.

THE GERMAN shepherd continued to ignore me. Every night he sat outside the train station, waiting, and didn't recognize me when I arrived. Ed knew the dog too, and reported that when he came home each night, two or three hours after me, the dog was still waiting. Ed would stop and pet the big fellow and he recognized Ed as he always had—it was only me whom he didn't know anymore.

"Where have you been?" It was James Cronin. A Monday afternoon at Fields & Carmine. James had the desk next to mine and we had never gotten along. With James everything was a competition; now he wanted to start about who took a shorter lunch.

"The coffee shop," I told him, "getting a hamburger."

"For two hours?" James asked, raising his eyebrows.

I rolled my eyes at him. "What two hours? I left at one and now it's—" I looked at my watch. Three o'clock. That couldn't be right. I bent down to look at the clock on James's desk. They jibed. Three o'clock.

My mind took a step backwards and then forwards, trying to make sense of the situation. I had gone to Pete's for a burger, then to the magazine stand on the corner, then back to work. I had looked at my watch on the way back and seen five to. One hour.

Impossible. But here I was. James was looking at me with his big gray eyes. I felt as if the ground underneath me was no longer stable but tilting, one way and then the other. My mind stopped to rearrange itself. I went into an emergency mode where the first thing was to deal with James Cronin.

"Oh, yeah, I did leave at one," I told James, as if I hadn't said it a moment before with an entirely different tone. "I had some errands."

I turned and sat down at my own desk. I went over the hour—no, two hours—in my mind again. First I had gone to the coffee shop for a hamburger. There was the usual waitress, the tired brunette. While I ate I read the newspaper, which I left in the coffee shop when I was done. Then I went to the magazine stand on the corner, down the block. I looked through a few women's magazines before I picked up *Architectural Record*. There was a little piece on my firm in the New and Noteworthy column. Of course we had a copy at the office but I wanted to show Ed. I checked my watch, twenty to two. Plenty of time. I flipped through a few women's magazines, a guilty pleasure. And then:

"Hey, hey. You can't read those here. Buy or don't buy. No reading."

I turned. It was the man running the shop.

"Well I AM buying, I'm getting this and I'm deciding about these others." I was angry, but only for a second or two. Ridiculous man. How could people know what to buy if they didn't look first? I thought of the utter absurdity of the situation: a man who was talking customers out of shopping in his store. Probably went home every night wondering why he didn't sell more magazines.

And then again: "Buy or don't buy. Come on, lady." I would have walked out but I had been looking for that

62

magazine for a week now; it was mostly sold by subscription and wasn't easy to find at a newsstand. I went to the counter.

"You know you're very rude. How is a person supposed to shop without looking around first?" I paid with five dollar bills and two quarters.

"You don't like it, get out. I don't need this."

I got angrier. All I wanted were a few magazines and here was this abuse. "I am getting out, and I won't come back."

I turned and left. I heard him behind me: "Fucking bitch."

I ignored him. What a nut. How does a person like that come to run a business? I lit a cigarette and smoked a few drags. I was still angry, even though I was embarrassed about it. It should be beneath me, taking this moronic woman-hater seriously.

I checked my watch. Fifteen minutes left. If I walked the long way back to work, took the streets instead of the avenue, that would fill the time nicely. I could smoke another cigarette and relax. Stressful morning, trouble with the electricians at the Fitzgerald house, and now this ridiculous fight with a stranger. I was about to step into the street when a woman rushed by, or maybe a man with long hair, lightning fast, and almost knocked me down. I stumbled, and then caught myself. Fucking messengers.

And then a dip. I had closed my eyes for a second,

a blink in anticipation of being hit by the messenger. I closed my eyes and there was a dip, a dip or a drop out of consciousness. I had a cigarette in my hand, the air smelled hot and dirty on the street corner, the messenger rushed by, I lost my balance, stumbled and then, I could just barely remember it, I saw black and lost the feeling of my feet on the ground.

It passed as quickly as it came, and there I was in front of the magazine store on the corner. The cigarette was gone. Of course you don't usually remember putting out a cigarette, not at a pack a day. That's twenty times a day you put out a cigarette.

Where was the magazine? I looked around my desk. Not there. In my mind I went back again to the magazine stand. After the messenger raced by I shook my head, took a second to get my bearings. Just a little moment of light-headedness. I walked up the side streets back to work, smoked another cigarette, stopped to admire a beautiful red rose bush in a front yard. I stopped to check my watch before I came back into the building. Five to. What I expected. But I had only checked the long minute hand, not the short hour hand. So where was the magazine? I didn't have it on the way back to work. I remembered reaching into my purse for cigarettes and lighter and having both hands free. No cigarette, no magazine.

I mulled it over in my mind for a few minutes before I came up with an answer: I had fainted. That was the only possibility. When I thought I had only stumbled, avoiding the messenger, I had fainted. I had been out for an hour, righted myself, and then returned to work without knowing it had happened, drawing no attention from a single passerby, and then forgotten the whole thing. Sitting at my desk I weighed a visit to the emergency room. No, I was okay now.

It was just like people in this city not to stop and help. Of course the magazine dealer would have seen the whole thing through the door, but he certainly wouldn't have lifted a finger to help me. I called Edward at the office but he was out. The rest of the day went by without incident and at six I went home. There was a message from Ed on the answering machine saying he would be late again. I ate a bowl of cereal at the kitchen table and almost forgot about having fainted—until I went to the bedroom and started to undress, changing into pajamas for the evening. Underneath my jacket, on the left shoulder of my white shirt, was a spray of small brown dots.

It looked like blood. Enough so, in fact, that there was nothing it could be but blood. My mind flip-flopped again. Then I remembered lunch at the coffee shop—a rare hamburger. Mystery solved. The stain was from lunch. I had transmitted a fine spray of blood from a cooked hamburger around my jacket and onto the shoulder of the shirt underneath, then I had fainted, righted myself, and forgotten about it. As simple as that.

Edward came home at nine, with a bag of Mexican take-out for dinner and an armload of apologies. I told him what had happened and, shocked, he quizzed me with all the warmth of an emergency room doctor: What had I eaten? Was I getting my period? Had I slept well last night? How did I feel now?

"Why are you interrogating me?" I yelled. I felt fine, I looked fine, eventually I convinced him that I was fine.

It wasn't until a few days later that I happened to watch the television news. Ed was still at work. The sun had just gone down and a gray light was coming through the windows, meeting the blue from the television in the middle of the room. I was sitting on the sofa about to bite into another take-out dinner, pad thai and papaya salad.

A vaguely familiar face popped up on the television screen. Middle-aged, male, not at all attractive. Where did I know him from?

"Kareem Singh was buried today," a woman's voice said. Cut to a funeral in a crowded slum of the city. "The owner of a newsstand was killed with a box cutter on Monday afternoon in what police think was an attempted robbery."

Of course. The asshole from the magazine stand. Horrible. But I wasn't surprised, the way he'd acted. Probably said the wrong thing to the wrong person. And I had been there on Monday, it must have been right before—

For a very small moment, for a tiny sliver of time, the thought occurred to me. But as soon as the spark was lit it was put out again. Impossible. The television news moved on, cut-cut, and so did I.

It wasn't until months later that I would look back and realize that, most likely, I had killed the magazine dealer myself.

That weekend we went to the Asian Museum to see a rare display of Meiji Japanese furniture, Edward's favorite. After we walked through the exhibit we had an elegant lunch in the museum cafe, watercress salad and crustless salmon sandwiches—a little too elegant, I guess, because soon afterwards we were hungry again, and went for a walk in the park in search of hot dogs and pretzels.

In the park we ran into Alex and Sophia and their six-year-old daughter, Claire. I didn't like Alex and Sophia. All that could annoy me about Ed was amplified in Alex and Sophia. They worked in finance, in some capacity, and made tons of money. Their apartment was revoltingly spotless and bland with an absurd white carpet they paid a woman to come in and scrub twice a week.

Luckily they had Claire, so I had some entertainment when we met. While Ed and his friends talked about Alex's promotion, which was supposed to be interesting, Claire and I walked down to the lake to look at the swans. Swans were beautiful but could be dangerous, I explained to Claire as we walked. As long as they didn't feel threatened, I told her, they were fine. But if we were to get too close to the birds they would try to bite.

When we got to the water we stood there for a minute or two, watching four white swans pick each other's feathers clean with their hard orange beaks. Then Claire turned to me—not exactly to me but in my direction, a little to my left. She did this a few more times, and I looked around to see if anything interesting was going on. But I knew a little girl could find an unusual blade of grass or an out-of-place bottle cap fascinating, so I didn't give it too much thought.

Then Claire turned towards me again. "Are you sure?" she asked.

"Sure about what, honey?" I said.

She ignored me. "Okay," Claire said. And then she let go of my hand and ran to the water's edge and reached her hand out to the nearest swan. The bird bent its long neck towards Claire with a nasty look on its face. It all happened in the blink of an eye. I ran down after Claire, scooped her up, and jumped back. The bird waddled up the riverbank after us.

"Hey!" I yelled at the swan. "Fuck off!" It stopped and stared with its beady eyes. I ran with Claire in my arms like a sack of potatoes back up the embankment. After a few yards I put her down and we walked back towards her parents.

"Claire, why did you do that?"

She squeezed her eyebrows together and pouted. "She told me to!" she cried. "She said I could!"

"What are you talking about? No one told you to do anything."

"Her!" Claire said with frustration. She pointed to my left side, at about the same angle she had been looking earlier. "Your friend."

"Who, honey?"

"The lady who's always with you," she said. Claire pouted and looked at the ground.

When we got back to our little group I told Sophia that Claire had been telling lies.

THAT NIGHT I picked up *Demon Possession Past and Present* and took the quiz again. This time I scored a seven.

0–3: You are probably not possessed. See a doctor or mental health professional for an evaluation.

3–6: You may be haunted, or in the early stages of possession. Do not be alarmed. Seek a spiritual counselor for assistance.

6–10: You are possessed. Consult with your spiritual counselor immediately. You may be a threat to the safety of yourself and your family. See the RESOURCES page for a qualified professional in your area.

S ister Maria, spiritual advisor, was the closest professional in my area. What could it hurt? I asked
myself. I had always been curious to visit a psychic,
just to see how they did it—the tricks they might use, the
leading questions—because of course there was nothing
to it. Of course I didn't believe in psychics or spiritualists
or demons or devils. At the very best this Maria might be
an intelligent person with strong intuition who could give
me a little insight into the changes that I saw happening
in myself the past few months. *Take some time to relax*, I
imagined she would tell me. *Take some vitamin C*. At the
worst, it would be good for a laugh. I used that phrase
a lot that year, *good for a laugh*. And the word *curious*.
That's what I would tell Ed if he found out that I wasn't
at the Fitzgerald house that day, like I had told him—it
was just for a laugh, I would tell him. I was curious.

In the northern tip of the city, where Sister Maria's shop
or office or clinic was, I didn't know what to expect—the
streets crunched with bottle caps and fast-food wrap-
pers and used hypodermic needles. The windows in the
rundown tenements were cracked, some missing and
replaced with balsa wood or particleboard. But it wasn't

wholly without charm: an elderly man sat on a folding chair in front of his doorway, hat in hand, and wished me a fine day. On a grocery store wall I noticed a small plaque from the Landmarks Commission; it had been the site of a famous jazz nightclub in the thirties. A slow, wailing big band sound flowed through an open window. *Accompaneme*, the woman sang—come with me. A crowd of children played hopscotch in the middle of a street. Up the street a clique of teenage girls sat on a stoop and pretended to ignore the grandstanding teenage boys on the street around them.

At number 77 was a shop with a life-sized plaster Madonna in the window. She wore a black wig and a white dress, and at her feet was a bowl of water with coins at the bottom. The glass was clean and the street in front was well swept. A bell jangled when I opened the door. Inside was a neat little shop lined with shelves like a grocery store, except I wasn't quite sure what was on the shelves. Jars of herbs. Quarts of green and brown liquids labeled with numbers. Come-to-me oil, money-drawing soap, house-blessing spray, hot-foot powder, four thieves vinegar, Florida Water, St. Christopher oil. Candles in the shape of men, women, cats, and dogs. Lucite pyramids filled with lucky charms, and good old-fashioned crystal balls in various sizes. Behind a glass case of medallions and charms stood a teenage boy, a flaming queer in tight designer jeans with a silver ring through his bottom lip. He smiled and asked if he could help me.

74

"I'm here for, uh, to see Sister Maria."

He went to the back of the shop, opened a door, and called out in a language I had never heard before—Portuguese, maybe—but somehow I knew what it meant.

"A white woman's here to see you," he called. "I've never seen her before."

"Send her in right away," the woman called back. "Then lock up and go to lunch."

THE BACK room was pretty much what I expected a low-rent reading room to look like; walls draped in deep red velveteen, a folding card table with more velveteen draped over it, anchored in place with a crystal ball, a cup for reading tea leaves, a pen and paper, and a deck of tarot cards. At the table sat a woman five or ten years older than me, with nutmeg skin and pretty features hidden behind cheap makeup. She wore blue jeans and a tight denim jacket. She gestured for me to sit in a folding chair across the table from hers. I sat down.

I was curious. It would be good for a laugh.

"What's you name?" she asked. I told her. She wrote it down on the paper and did a quick calculation.

"You number is seven," she said. She took the deck of tarot cards and laid seven of them out on the table. Death, The Tower, Queen of Pentacles, The Moon, Five of Swords, Eight of Swords, The Lovers. I had no idea what any of them meant. Maria looked at the cards for a few minutes, then back up to me with her eyebrows pushed together, then down at the cards again.

"Someone's watching you," she finally said. "She's right next to you. Beautiful, but black. Evil. Have you tried to get rid of her?"

This wasn't so good for a laugh. This was less funny by the moment. "Who is it?" I asked.

"It's not a who," Maria answered. "It's a what. A demon. I see her; she has long black hair and pointy teeth."

"Are you sure she's a demon?"

Maria nodded. "No one else has a black aura like that. So you haven't tried to get rid of it?"

I shook my head. "I didn't know."

"You really didn't know what that was?" Maria asked. Her voice was suspicious. I had a sick nervous feeling as she looked at me; it reminded me of being in school without having done my homework. I felt like I had been caught at something naughty.

"No," I told her. "How was I supposed to know?"

Maria looked at me crook-eyed again, like she wasn't quite buying my excuse. "You have to do exactly as I say, it's very important. I'm going to give you a wash. Number Five. For three nights in a row you pour it over yourself while you pray. Pray to God to help you. Then you stop for three days, then you use it again for three days. Use it until the bottle's all gone. It won't make her disappear but it will cleanse your spirit so you can fight her better. But the most important thing is that you never, ever give in. You give even an inch, she'll take a hundred miles."

"What if it doesn't work?" I asked.

"It always works."

"But what if it doesn't?"

"She'll possess you. She's probably already started. Not all at once. You won't lose yourself all at once. But a little bit at a time. That's why you have to do exactly as I say."

"I understand," I promised.

Maria stood up and I was clearly dismissed. Out in the store I settled the bill with the young man who had come back and was eyeing me curiously. He handed me a large jug of thin, greenish gray liquid in which floated a few leaves and twigs and some small berries that looked like peppercorns. On a white label with black letters was printed: "NUMBER #5: DEMON FIGHTING."

SISTER MARIA had held me spellbound, but back at home it was easy for the whole matter to be good for a laugh again. Except I wasn't laughing, and I didn't tell anyone else about it, either. But I thought I might as well use the wash. I mean, it couldn't hurt. It's not like it would do anything, of course, but it wouldn't hurt. I rubbed off the neatly typed label with vegetable oil, so if Ed noticed the bottle I could tell him it was bubble bath. I stood in the bathtub, naked, and asked God to help me as I poured the liquid over my head. It smelled like licorice, and it stung slightly where it dripped into my eyes. I kept my mouth closed so I wouldn't swallow anything—I had

77

forgotten to ask about that. I spread out my arms and let the wash trickle down my body, leaving a trail of goose bumps where it flowed.

Nothing happened. I wasn't sure if I was supposed to rinse afterwards or just let it dry on my skin, but it smelled strong and so I took a quick warm shower, and then dried off and put on pajamas and spent the rest of the night paying bills and watching television.

The German Shepherd was waiting at the train station again a few days later, looking right through me. The idiot didn't even know who I was anymore. "Go," I snapped. "Get out of here."

The dog looked at me and I looked back. I really hated him now, this stupid beast, staring at me with those big chocolate accusatory eyes.

"Go," I yelled again. I pointed toward the wasteland of our neighborhood, in the opposite direction from our house. Still holding my eyes, he pulled his shoulders down and his tail up, as if he were stretching his back. Then he leapt up to my outstretched hand and bit me.

I screamed, more from shock than pain. The skin on my hand was barely punctured, and it felt more like a book had been dropped on my hand than what I had imagined a dog bite would feel like. Then he lay down with his head between his paws and whimpered. Now, finally, the old adage had become true. He *was* more scared of me than I was of him.

"Fuck off!" I screamed. The idiot got up and ran away. I went home, washed my hand, wrapped it in a clean white dish towel, and called Ed, hoping he would drive me to the emergency room. He wasn't in, so I called a taxi to take me instead. By the time I got to the hospital it hurt at least as much as I had imagined a dog bite would. I tried Ed again. Still out. For three hours I sat in the waiting room and tried to guess what the other people waiting had wrong with them. Some were obvious—hacking coughs, swollen appendages—but most I had to guess. Finally I was ushered into a brightly lit little examination cubicle, where a doctor washed the wound and then asked if I knew the dog who had bit me.

"Why?" I asked.

"Because if you don't, you need to get two shots now, another in three days, another in seven, another in fourteen, and another in twenty-eight. Whenever there's a bite by an unknown dog, there's a chance of rabies."

"What if I'm really, really sure this dog doesn't have rabies?" I asked.

"If you don't know the dog," he said with irritation, "you're not really, really sure. The only way to avoid the shots is to get a brain sample from the dog. Now this is going to hurt."

The doctor gave me a shot with a thick needle in my right hand, near the bite, and then another shot in the upper arm. The shots hurt worse than the bite had.

It was obvious that a brain sample couldn't come from a living dog. *Good*, I thought at first, *serves the stupid fucker right*. Then I thought of that dumb old dog, the fellow who used to be my pal, my best buddy, how he never gave up trying to seduce me, even after I made it clear I was married. I couldn't. So on the third, seventh, fourteenth, and twenty-eighth day after the bite I went to the doctor's office for more painful shots, and I never saw the dog again.

ED WAS in a state when I got home at eleven that night, furious that I had let him worry. When I explained where I had been and showed him the ugly red puncture marks on my hand he relented and showed appropriate sympathy.

"Really, though," he said, after kissing my hand, "you should have called."

We were sitting on the sofa, curled up close. He gently held my bitten hand. For a few minutes we had been in love again. Friends again. And now this. *He wants an apology*, I thought. "I tried," I told him. "Twice."

"Still, hon, I was worried."

Where was he? I thought. "I tried," I said. "Where were you, anyway?"

Ed made a face. "What do you mean, where was I? Working, you know that."

"Just asking. You ought to get one of those cellular phones. In case of an emergency. You're out of the office so much these days."

Ed rolled his eyes. "I'm always out of the office a lot, Amanda, that's half my job. You know that."

Then why not get a phone? "Then why not get a phone?"

"Why, so you can keep tabs on me?"

"No, not so I can keep tabs on you. So if I get bitten by a rabid dog you can drive me to the emergency room."

Ed dropped my hand. "Do you plan on doing this often? Bothering stray animals and then getting rabies? Because if so, maybe we can get you vaccinated or something."

We sat stiffly on the sofa, side-by-side now. "Yes, Ed," I told him. "I plan on doing this often."

When I went to Dr. Flynn for my seventh day rabies shot, the story about fainting a few weeks before at the magazine stand came out. Dr. Flynn was my age and blonde. She had been Ed's doctor for years. The first time I saw her, the day after my trip to the emergency room, I was immensely jealous. She wasn't who I would have picked to examine my naked husband. But my own doctor, Jeff Winston, had died of a stroke two months before, and Ed raved about Dr. Flynn.

She gave me a full physical, took blood for testing, and interrogated me for half an hour about the day I had fainted. What had I eaten? When had I eaten it? Did I have any strange food cravings? Strange dreams? Irrational thoughts? Had I been exposed to any toxic chemicals? On and on.

At the end of all the questions and tests and needles and samples she said I had low blood pressure and ought to eat more salt. I liked the sound of Dr. Flynn's diagnosis. Everything could be explained, my life could go on. All I needed was more salt.

I took the fact that Sister Maria's potion had done nothing as proof that there had never been anything wrong. Of course it had only been for a laugh, anyway. Just out of curiosity. But the dreams about a woman on a red beach continued just the same. And Ed and I continued to fight, and I kept doing things like snapping at cab drivers and occasionally going back for a drink to the bar where I had drunk all that tequila. A heat wave came over the city and everyone was on edge. Ed would come home each night and complain about the heat and I wanted to kill him. I knew it was hot. I didn't need to talk about it.

Occasionally I thought about how much I had changed over the past few months and I was able to take a step back and look at the situation and I was horrified. The old Amanda, the one I had chosen for myself and cultivated for years, would rear her head and scream.

Just when I was on the verge of seeing the truth, when the pieces would start to fall into place and I could almost see that the situation was horribly, drastically, wrong, the demon's voice would step in and tell me No, I was the same Amanda I had always been. Only better.

T hen there was the Earmark Hotel party. The Earmark was a Jet-set hotel downtown. Fields & Carmine had remodeled the lobby, restaurant, and bar, and we were all invited to the reopening party. Ed, naturally, had to work late that night, so I took a cab down with the other single people from the office.

I was planning to just stay for a few drinks, fulfill my obligations as a Fields & Carmine staff member, and then take off. But the party was swinging and the hotel was packed, and clearly there would be no quick in and out. The people I had come with drifted away. I found myself talking to Tom and Bill Earmark, the brothers who owned the hotel. I barely knew them—we had made a little small talk in the office and I had sat in on a few meetings. But very quickly Tom was taking me behind the bar for a martini he made himself, to avoid the line, and showing me around the new space. He took my arm to lead me through the crowd, and when he touched my arm I had a flash of intuition—*He likes you, he always has, from the first time he saw you in the office, walking in the door with a sunburn across the bridge of your nose and your hair down.*

Then everything got kind of blurry. I was talking to Tom. His eyes, which had always been good, big and clear and bluish gray, got better and better. We drank martinis but I wasn't getting drunk. I was becoming less there. I was sliding away. I was talking to Tom, I didn't know what we were talking about, and his eyes were getting better and better, and so were his cheekbones—irresistible, really—and I was talking, not just talking but flirting, horribly flirting, putting my hand on Tom's forearm and then on his shoulders, tossing my head back when I laughed. But I wasn't there. I was watching it all, I could see it, but I wasn't inside of myself. It was all so muddled—I caught snippets of conversation and odd sensations, like a strong smell of gin, the feel of the loud music pounding in my chest. I was watching a movie too late at night, half-asleep, not grasping the plot at all. We were talking and laughing, and then I got a tour of the empty kitchen, alone. Then we were getting into an elevator together. His arm was around my shoulder. I thought maybe I was here, in this elevator with Tom, but I could be in a different place. I could be a different person. I tried to get hold of the situation, to see for sure exactly who and where I was, but I couldn't get my hands around it, the situation kept slipping out from my grasp and I was left wondering, unsure.

We were in the penthouse. It was a great little space, separate bedroom off to one side, really modern and spare, all neutral colors, and of course, there was that great relaxing hotel anonymity. It was like looking at a photograph, seeing the room but not being in it. And then we were on the sofa with a bottle of wine and then we were in bed. Tom was beautiful without clothes. Tom screamed, he said my name, I saw red and heard a roar in my ears like an ocean, I didn't know who or where I was . . .

And then it was over. I was back solidly in my own body, completely present, sure of myself and my surroundings. I sat on the edge of the bed, naked and shivering. Tom lay on the bed, snoring a revolting drunken snort. I was disgusted. My stomach turned. How, I asked myself, how—how—how did this happen? A filthy horrible thing. The most filthy horrible thing I had ever done. As quickly as I could I put on my clothes and ran out to the street, where I vomited once in the gutter and then got a taxi to take me home.

WANDERING THE aisles of a brightly lit supermarket in the city the next evening I couldn't get the night before off my mind. In the meat aisle I stopped and looked at the steaks. I would make Ed his favorite dinner tonight, steak with mushroom sauce, and I would start again, retrain myself to see him as my husband, the man I had chosen to love and respect for the rest of my life. All this nonsense had to end. We fought almost every day now. In a rare lucid moment I saw that we were dissolving as a couple, and if I didn't stop it now there would be nothing to save.

I was comparing prices on T-bones when the demon slithered back into my thoughts. *Make dinner?* she said. *Hours in the kitchen and then he won't even come home on time and will never appreciate it. Besides, Ed hasn't cooked for you in ages, not since that horrible string bean mess he concocted months and months ago.*

I dropped the steak back into its bin, abandoned my cart, and left the supermarket. The rest of the evening was spent shopping for shoes. The demon loved to shop. Two or three times a week I would take out my credit card for little luxuries that later, at home, confused me. Why had I bought a leather jacket when I already had two in my closet? What made me think I needed a red cocktail dress?

I came home that night with three pairs of high-heeled pumps and nothing to eat. When Ed came home at eight, only one hour later than promised, we had a terrible fight over why I hadn't brought home dinner, which, he reminded me, I had said I would do.

THE NEXT day I went to a bookstore, a big multilevel place, airless and empty so early in the day. I browsed a few titles; psychic fine tuning, chakra realignment, aura cleansing.

"Can I help you?"

It was the voice of an adult woman, not the usual bookstore clerk squeak.

"No, thanks." I looked up with a smile. But no one was there. I turned in a circle and looked through the whole aisle. No one.

Back to the books. I looked at a few more titles. And then—

"Are you looking for something?"

I spun around as quickly as I could. No one. Over the top of the next shelf I saw the tip of a head, with thick dark hair, quickly darting through the next aisle.

Behind me I heard a bang. I screamed and jumped, turning around. The crash was just a book that had fallen down from a top shelf and onto the floor. Immediately I felt like an idiot. Just a book. Two young clerks came running over, a boy and a girl.

"Are you okay?" squeaked the boy.

"Yes, I just—it fell. It surprised me. Sorry."

The girl bent down to pick up the book. *The Encyclopedia of Demons.*

"Actually," I said. "Can I—"

"Sure," the girl said. She handed me the book. I added it to the pile I already had, paid, and went home to pack; the next morning we were going away, to Alex and Sophia's beach house for the weekend, and Ed wanted to leave early to beat the traffic.

Although it wasn't discussed, it was clear that Ed and I would both be on our best behavior this weekend, and get our relationship back on track. Saturday morning it seemed like it would be easy. It was a brilliant day, the sun was still summery yellow and warm, and we listened to a rock and roll marathon on the radio as we drove out. Ed sang along with the radio in a silly voice; I took off my shoes and rested my newly pedicured feet on the dashboard. We rolled down the windows and the sun shone into the car. When Ed's hand wasn't needed on the steering wheel, he put it in my lap.

Alex and Sophia's house was as bland as they were: lots of pale blue throw pillows and store-bought sea-shells scattered around. But it was neat and comfortable, and most important, it was steps from the beach. At the house I changed into a black one-piece swimsuit and Ed put on his loose khaki trunks that went almost to his knees. After a quick look around the house to check for necessities—soap, shampoo, towels, coffee—we walked down to the beach and settled in on a worn pink bedsheet we had brought from home. Ed took out a paperback novel, and after a few pages fell asleep, snoring on the sheet next to me. I lay down and tried to nap.

But I couldn't fall asleep. The sun was too hot, the small patch of sheet was confining, and Edward was annoying, snoring as he was. I was burning hot. I decided to go for a swim.

I stood up and walked towards the water. Officially, the season had ended. No lifeguards were out and swimming wasn't allowed but no one was there to stop the handful of us who bobbed in and out of the shallow water.

I swam up and down a few yards of the ocean, and then out a little further. The water was still shallow enough so that I could stand. I closed my eyes and felt the cold of the water and the heat of the sun. When I opened my eyes I saw a little girl, maybe five or six, a few feet away, between me and the shore. She shouldn't have been in the water alone at all, let alone out so far. Ordinarily I would have led her back to the shore. Today, though, I just watched her. She splashed happily around in the small waves, dunking her head in and out and letting her small body get tossed around by the gentle undertow. Her nutmeg skin was sunburned red on the shoulders. She saw me watching her and smiled. I smiled back.

"You shouldn't be out so deep," I said. She shrugged and dunked under again. A little wave came in and tossed her around. I saw the top of her head poke up from the water, then her tiny feet. When she finally righted herself and got her head above water she was coughing, maybe crying a little. Not hurt, but scared.

"I'll help you," I said. I swam towards her. While I was on my way another little wave came along, knocking her down again. I dove towards her and then reached out and grabbed her hair, as if to pull her head above water.

But I didn't. I grabbed her hair in my right hand and pulled down. Sickeningly, I could feel the life drain from her as I held her under the water, feel the heat from her body trickle away. I saw her life before my eyes, most of it lived in a cramped railroad apartment. Just before she drowned I pulled her up and let her take some air, then pulled her back down again. It was a game. Up down, up down. The girl had a head on her shoulders though, and the next time up she started to scream. A fat middle-aged woman swimming near the shore perked her head up and looked around. I plunged the girl under one more time and dunked my own head too, as if we'd both been caught in an undercurrent, and then jumped back up with my arm around the girl's head.

"I think she's drowning," I called out to the woman, who was quickly walking through the water towards us. "Give me a hand." The strong woman grabbed the limp child out of my arms and ran with her towards the shore. I ran after her.

Back on the warm sand the child started crying, which was a good sign that no permanent damage had been done. The commotion woke up Ed and he came running down to where a small crowd had formed around the girl. She sat up, looked around, and threw up a stomach full of salt water—another good sign, the crowd agreed. The girl's mother came running, crying and screaming, as if she hadn't done worse to her daughter at home. I had seen it all.

"You saved my baby's life!" she cried to the older woman and me. The older woman looked at me oddly but said nothing. I could imagine her telling herself that of course I had been pulling her out, not pushing her in. That must have been what she saw. I must have been pulling her out. The girl herself was still in a mild shock. If she were ever to tell anyone that I had been trying to end her life, not save it, I was sure no one would believe her.

The older woman went off to the spot where her fat husband was waiting. The crying mother took her crying daughter back to their blanket. Edward took my hand and led me back to our own pink sheet, where we sat down and I started to cry myself.

"Shh." He wrapped his arms around me. "Everyone's fine. You must have been terrified, poor baby."

I looked up at the sky. A flock of birds was circling high above us, flying in and out of a V formation. One by one they left the V and then regrouped, flying into place one at a time to spell out a name, perfectly as a pen on paper.

NAAMAH.

BACK AT the house Ed took the car and drove out to the bay to buy dinner, fresh steamer clams and corn on the cob, which he cooked himself. He asked me what I thought of dinner and if I was having a good time and I just kept saying "Mmm," which he took as a positive response.

After dinner we lay on the sofa. We had been planning on going back to the beach for the sunset but I needed to rest. After a few minutes Ed fell asleep again. I went to the bedroom and got out *The Encyclopedia of Demons*, which I had hidden in the bottom of my bag. With a sick feeling in my stomach I flipped through until I got to the N's. There she was, with a few pages in *The Encyclopedia of Demons* all to herself.

NAAMAH

The most famous stories of Naamah come from the Kabala, the Jewish mystical texts formerly available in full only to Jewish male scholars over the age of forty. Her name is thought to mean "charming" or "pleasant" in her native Aramaic, a reference to her desirability to men. Due to the occult nature of Kabalic wisdom, there may be much more attached to the name than we can know; especially one wonders about its origins and its numerological significance. Like most of her type, she is made stronger by water (especially salt water), sexual desire, and other impure thoughts.

Naamah's story begins at the beginning of time, as Adam's second wife: Adam's first wife was Lilith. While Adam was made from pure earth she was made from filth and sediment, and she could not be a mate for Adam. Adam wanted Lilith to be submissive, but Lilith refused, and she went to live by the Red Sea and became the mother of all demons. So God made a second wife, Naamah, and this one he made in front of Adam, starting from scratch, in order to meet Adam's specifications. He started with the bones, then the organs, then the muscles, blood, et cetera, and by the time God was done, Adam was so disgusted he would have nothing to do with her. And Naamah, along with Lilith, was banished to the banks of the Red Sea. In another story, Naamah's origins are vague but her purpose clearer. After Cain kills Abel, Adam is so horrified by his children that he refuses to sleep with Eve for over one hundred years. During this time, Naamah comes to him in his sleep and, preying on his dreams, impregnates herself with his semen. This is the source of the Jewish preference that men, especially rabbis and scholars, be married—unless a man made love to his wife regularly, what he thought was a simple nocturnal emission could really be a demon making love to him, impregnating herself with his seed. In Genesis, we see Naamah yet again. In this story she's the daughter of Lamach and Zillah. This Naamah wasn't a demon, just a human. But oddly enough, this Naamah married her brother, Tubal Cain, and then gave birth to a demon—Asmodeus, who we still know today. Hence her reputation as a fierce and proud mother, whose secondary goal—after seduction—is to eliminate any children that are not her own. In Kings 3:16, she appears again (along with Lilith), as one of the two harlots sent to test the wisdom of Solomon. Posing as two mothers arguing over the maternity of a child, the demons attempt to trick Solomon into making a foolish decision; instead, Solomon offers to cut the child in half, knowing the true mother will give up her claim. Defeated, the two demons go back to whence they came. As with all stories concerning Solomon, this myth figures in Freemasonry legend as well.

In addition to these, there are far more instances of Naamah's unfortunate influence throughout Christian and Jewish history.

The next morning I told Edward I didn't feel well—sun poisoning—and that I ought to stay home while he went to the beach. Once he was gone I read some more from the book:

If only the average person knew the early warning signs of possession, much heartbreak could be averted. The most common first sign is an unusual noise in the household, perhaps a scratching, a tapping, or footsteps ... Once inside its victim the demon will usually start off with small mischief—petty

97

theft, arguments, and the like. Its usual MO is to slowly work its way to a stronghold over the victim before revealing its true nature, thus insuring it will not be recognized and exorcised while its grip is still weak. Unfortunately, we see and hear of too many cases where, by the time the demon is discovered, the victim is so far under its control that he or she cannot be brought in for a voluntary exorcism. The chances of recovery from possession in these cases are small.

Ed came back from the beach that afternoon in a wonderful mood. He wanted us to drive out to a seafood restaurant on the bay that he had seen the day before.

"I still don't feel well," I told him. "I want to stay in bed."

He pouted. "Hon, come on, this is supposed to be our vacation."

"I don't want to," I said. "I feel like shit. Ed, I think I—"

Ed, I think I'm going crazy, I was going to say. *I think I'm possessed.* But he cut me off.

"Christ!" he said. "Can't we ever have any fun anymore? Can't we even have one fucking nice weekend at the beach?"

He scowled. The demon's voice screamed in my head, and the next thing I knew I was screaming at Ed.

"You want to have *fun*!" I shouted. "LOOK at me!"

"I just wanted—"

"YOU wanted! All you think about is yourself! Can't

you see I'm sick, can't you see there's something WRONG WITH ME? YOU'RE SO FUCKING SELFISH!"

By now I was standing on top of the bed, and I caught sight of myself in the mirror on top of the bureau across the room. My arms were flailing like an animal's, my eyes were wide, my lips dark pink, and my hair in knots, almost dreadlocks.

I looked just like her.

Ed stood in the doorway, disgusted. He turned and walked out of the house.

I collapsed on the bed and started to sob. *You see*, the satiny voice told me, *this is how much he cares. This is the huge love you were so proud of. The one you thought would last forever.*

Ed, however, suffered from no confusion whatsoever. He came back late that night, hours after I had been pretending to be asleep, and went to bed on the sofa without even checking the bedroom to see if I was alive.

When I woke up the next morning he was already awake, sheepishly drinking a cup of coffee at the kitchen table. I sheepishly joined him.

"Hey."

"Hi."

"I love you." He said it first.

"I love you too." I started to cry.

"Oh honey," he said. He scooted his chair closer to mine and put his arm around my shoulder. "Honey, did you ever think—I mean, you just seem so unhappy lately—maybe it's me, it just seems—I just think—well, maybe you could find someone to talk to. You know, like a therapist or something."

I looked up at Edward and saw his worried face and a strong love swelled in my belly and spread through me. For a moment the love eclipsed the demon's snaking thoughts. A therapist! I loved the idea. I wasn't possessed—I was insane! I would go to a shrink, maybe even to a mental institution for a while, but that was preferable to the alternative. A mental disorder I could handle. I could work with it, accept it, and eventually cure it.

"You're right," I told Ed with a smile. "I think I'm going crazy."

"No, honey, I didn't mean crazy, I just meant—"

"No, it's okay. You're right, call it whatever you want. I'll call Dr. Flynn tomorrow and get the name of a shrink."

Ed smiled. I smiled. There we were, husband and wife, one crazy, we thought, and one sane, as happy as happy could be.

T he next morning I called Dr. Flynn first thing, and without giving her the details told her I needed an immediate visit with a psychiatrist. She gave me the phone number of Dr. Gerald Fenton, a personal friend of hers who, she assured me, was the best psychotherapist she knew.

"Tell him I sent you," she said before she hung up. "He's very selective. Booked for years. Tell him I sent you."

Dr. Fenton's receptionist told me he wouldn't have an appointment free for a new patient for at least a month, and I almost gave up before I remembered the magic words.

"Dr. Flynn sent me," I told her.

"Well *that's* different," she said. "Let's see . . . Come in today."

"When?" I asked.

"Whatever," she said. "You can come right now, if you like."

I liked it, and I went right away.

Dr. Fenton's office was in a prewar apartment building in a quiet part of town near the park. The streets were lined with trees and women with baby carriages. I smiled at the babies. None smiled back. No living creature looked at me favorably anymore—babies scowled, dogs growled, cats hissed, even chipmunks and squirrels ran away. And other adult humans—well, forget about that. Yet here I was on my way to a psychiatrist's office, trying to convince myself that I had a regular psychological problem.

At Dr. Fenton's building I got buzzed in by a doorman and was then ushered into his office by a young, fashionable receptionist. I was told Dr. Fenton would be with me in a moment. The room looked like I had always imagined a psychiatrist's office would: a leather and wood Eames armchair for the doctor, a leather department store sofa where the patient could sit or recline. An oak bookshelf with psychiatric texts was interspersed with pre-Columbian reproductions and a few African masks propped up on stands. A nice botanical print, lavender, on the wall. A window that looked out to the apartment building across the street.

In a moment or two the doctor arrived with a smile and a warm handshake. Like the office, he fit well with my preconceived notions. Bearded, fortyish, bifocals, plainly dressed in a beige cardigan, white button-down shirt, and black slacks.

"I'm Dr. Fenton."

"I'm Amanda."

He smiled. I smiled. We beamed at each other.

"So Amanda," he said. "Tell me about why you're here today."

I selectively told him about my strange behavior over the past two months. I told him about arguing with Ed, about the new voice in my head, about the messiness and the new attitude at work. I left out the part about the dog. I left out the part about burning Ed with the cigarette. I especially left out the part about the girl at the beach, which I had already convinced myself could not have happened. In my new, psychiatric world view, these were unrelated coincidences, with no relevance to the topic at hand. The doctor took notes on a yellow legal pad as I spoke.

"So," he said when I was done. "What's the problem?"

I looked at him. "Huh?"

"What is it about these changes that upsets you?"

"This isn't me. I mean of course it's *me*, it's not like it's someone else. What I mean is, it's not my usual personality. That's why I'm here."

"Well," he said, "it sounds to me like you're coming into your own. You're not a girl anymore, you're an adult woman and you need to become more assertive."

"But I fight with my husband," I said. "We're fighting all the time."

He gave me a slightly condescending look. "Fighting," he said, "is a part of any relationship. Fighting is a part of growth."

"But I'm not happy," I said. The snaky voice in my head agreed with the doctor. *Don't argue*, it said.

"That's a problem," the doctor said. "But maybe the problem is that you're resisting growth. The problem is that you're not being open to change."

"But what if I don't want to change like this? What if I don't like what I'm becoming?"

We're growing, the voice said. *We're becoming better and better.*

"You can't fight time," the doctor said. "Amanda, you're thirty-four years old. You're coming into your own."

"But I burned my husband," I blurted out.

"That was an accident," the doctor said. "You slipped. Maybe Edward's not what you think he is, maybe you need to reevaluate your relationship."

I hadn't told him about the incident with the cigarette. I also hadn't told him my age.

"How did you know?" I asked, getting nervous.

"Amanda, relax," he said. "Dr. Flynn sent over your records, it's all in here." He picked up an overstuffed manila folder from the table. "See?"

"I didn't tell Dr. Flynn about the cigarette."

He smiled. "Of course you did. It's right here in your file."

"Let me see that." I reached out my hand. The doctor pulled back.

"Confidential," he said.

"I never told her. Let me see that." My heart was racing. The doctor scooted back in his chair. I stood up and reached for the file, but with his other hand he seized my wrist and held it, hard. I looked at his face. No smile. No friendly sparkling eyes. He was utterly, deathly serious. I stepped back and he eased his grasp on my wrist, not letting go completely until I was two steps away. I grabbed my coat and purse off the couch beside me and left the office.

LATER, THOUGH, as I walked around the streets of the tree-lined neighborhood, I thought maybe I had been foolish. After all, Dr. Flynn could have told him everything that I hadn't. There was no reason to assume anything out of the ordinary was going on. Still, I didn't like him. What was all that talk about becoming myself? He didn't think I was crazy, and if I wasn't crazy, I was possessed. The next day, I would ask Dr. Flynn for a different recommendation, or get one from a friend.

I walked through the park, embarrassed. The fact that I had run out of the doctor's office like a baby didn't exactly boost my self-esteem. What did I think, that the doctor was some kind of a voodoo priest? A satanist, maybe? Really, I was an idiot. I walked down a path that led into a little forest. How had I come to this? How had I—

I heard a rustle of leaves from the trees on my left. I looked around and realized I was deep in the little forest. I didn't see another soul. I shouldn't have been there but it was too late to turn back now. There was nothing to do but go on to the other side. I picked up my pace and walked farther. I heard another rustle—this time on my right. And then a laugh. A woman's laugh coming from the clump of trees on my left, and then again from the bushes on my right. I started to walk quickly, and then run. The rustling of the trees and the woman's laugh followed. I ran until I couldn't run any farther and I had to stop, panting, to catch my breath. I looked around—it didn't seem like I had moved forward at all. Had I been running in place? The trees shook around me and the laughter rolled off them like ripe fruit. The noise was deafening. A thin sweat saturated my clothes.

"Hello?" I said. "Hello?"

But I already knew who it was. I would fight her, I told myself. I would find a way to fight her off, destroy her if I had to, first thing when I got home I would tell Ed and—

The noise stopped. The forest was absolutely quiet, except for my own heavy breathing. The trees around me were perfectly still. My muscles burned. I could barely stand.

I felt a hand on top of my head. I felt it ruffle my hair and softly brush down my right cheek and back up again. It worked its fingers through my hair and massaged my scalp. I started to cry. The hand started to push. It pushed me to my knees. Then it slid down to my lower back and shoved me onto my belly, grinding me into the rough concrete, until I moaned and gasped for air.

"Amanda," she whispered to me, "I really don't think Edward needs to know about this."

*

THAT EVENING, Ed still at the office, I consulted the RESOURCES section of *Demon Possession Past and Present* again. The second closest spiritual counselor was Dr. Ray Thomas, director and CEO of the Ray of Hope Fellowship.

"Located off Highway 55 North at Exit 12. Make a right at Domino's and then look for the Wendy's—The Ray of Hope Fellowship is in between Wendy's and Coconuts in the Newton Heritage Strip Mall," the book read.

The next morning I drove out to Highway 55, Exit 12, and looked for a Wendy's. The Ray of Hope Fellowship was a low one-story brick building recessed deep in the strip mall with a big sign in the lawn. WELCOME, the sign said. I parked in the lot out front and smoked a cigarette before I went in. It was a bright day and a group of boys were skateboarding in the Fellowship parking lot. MEGADEATH, their T-shirts said. METALLICA. ANTHRAX. I watched the boys and smoked for a few minutes before I got out of the car.

The doors to the Fellowship were open. Inside it looked vaguely like a church, although it just as easily could have been a corporate conference room. Rows of pews, or what could have been benches, faced an altar, or maybe a presentation stand. I walked up the center aisle. No one was around. Nothing seemed to be going on.

"Well, hey there."

I spun around. At the other end of the aisle was a man as nondescript as the building itself. His features were symmetrical and plain, not unattractive but not particularly engaging either.

"You startled me," I said. We walked towards each other and met in the center. "I'm looking for Ray Thomas."

"That's me," he said, extending a hand. He wore a plain gray suit. We shook. "Let's have a seat." We each sat in a pew on either side of the aisle.

"So," he said, loudly—the pews were a little too far apart for conversation—"let me guess. You think you're possessed by a demon."

I smiled and nodded. His tone of voice put it all in perspective. *So you think you're possessed*, it said. *Don't we all, from time to time.*

"I suppose you took that quiz," he continued. I nodded again. "And you answered yes to a few questions, and you got a little spooked, and now you think you're involved in some sort of *spiritual warfare*." He said the last two words with a flourish of his hands that implied hocus-pocus, circus tricks, voodoo. "Let me tell you, publishing that quiz was the dumbest thing we've ever done. I had no idea how many people there were out there with mental health conditions until the calls started flooding in. Not that you're one of them," he added. "Did you bring the book with you?"

I reached into my purse and took out the book, folded open to the quiz page.

"Now let's take a look," Ray Thomas said. We were both smiling, almost chuckling. He took the book and read my marked up quiz.

Are YOU Possessed by a Demon?

1. I hear strange noises in my home, especially at night, which family members tell me only occur when I am present. (I used to.)

2. I have new activities and pastimes that seem "out of character," and I do things that I did not intend and do not understand. (Yes.)

3. I'm short- and ill-tempered with my friends and loved ones. (Yes.)

4. I can understand languages I've never studied, and have the ability to know things I couldn't know through ordinary means. (Yes.)

5. I have blackouts not caused by drugs, alcohol, or a preexisting health condition. (Yes.)

6. I have unusual new thoughts, or hear voices in my head. (All the time.)

7. I've had visions or dreams of personalities who may be demons. (Yes.)

8. A psychic, minister, or other spiritualist has told me I'm possessed. (Yes.)

9. I have urges to hurt or kill animals and other people. (Yes.)

10. I have hurt or killed animals or people. (Yes, definitely hurt, maybe killed.)

Ray Thomas wasn't smiling at all anymore. In fact he was frowning.

"What did you say your name was?" he asked.

"Amanda," I told him.

"Amanda, what we have here is a ninety to one hundred percent chance that you're plagued by an unwanted entity. At the very least we can be one hundred percent sure there's some entity interference going on here. How do you feel about a depossession?"

"Depossession?"

"We don't use the e-word around here," said Ray Thomas. "Fills people's heads with all kinds of ideas. Depossession is a simple process of visualization, separation, and healing. It's the most natural thing in the world."

"Does it work?" I asked.

Ray Thomas smiled again, and nodded his head. "We have over a ninety percent success rate with our depossession treatments here at Ray of Hope."

"What about the other ten percent?" I asked.

"Seven percent. Don't worry about that now."

RAY THOMAS took me to an office where I signed a release form saying that the procedure I was about to undergo was for entertainment purposes only. Then he led me into a small room behind the altar. The room was lit by fluorescent lights. There was a hospital-type bed made up with white linens and a blue blanket against one wall and a steel desk with a padded rolling desk chair against the opposite wall. He instructed me to lie on the bed. He sat in the rolling chair and scooted over to the bedside, then pulled a chain and turned out the overhead fluorescent.

"We start by visualizing a clean, pure space. Can you visualize a clean, pure space, Amanda?"

"Sure," I said. I stared at the ceiling and thought of an empty white room. The room had tall windows with sheer white curtains, billowing in a sunny summer breeze.

"We visualize with our eyes closed," he said.

"Oh." I closed my eyes and the white room became much clearer.

"You're in your clean, pure space," he said. "You're relaxing in your space. You're breathing deeply."

I was lying on a feather bed on the floor of the white room in a pair of white pajamas. A little sunlight bled in from behind the curtains. The room smelled like honey and flowers. I was somewhat relaxed.

"You're completely safe and secure and comfortable. Nothing can hurt you and you have no fears while you're in your space."

I felt moderately secure and relatively safe.

"Now imagine your unwanted entity. Remember, your space is a safe space, and the entity is there as your guest. You are in control. He or she cannot hurt you in your space."

I sat up from the feather bed. Someone was in the room with me. I turned around. Naamah was crouched on the floor behind me at the head of the bed.

"Remember, you're in control here. This is your space, and you're in control of the situation."

Naamah laughed and scurried away, towards a corner of the room that had fallen dark. I couldn't see her but I knew she was there, in the shadows. I looked around the room. All the corners were dark now. She could be in any of them.

"Now imagine a thin silver cord connecting you to your entity."

I felt a yank in my stomach, a twisting like cramps. I looked down and saw a thick black cord, greasy and wet, extending from my pajamas and leading to the far corner of the room.

"In your hand you have a pair of scissors. These are very sharp scissors, and they can cut through anything you want them to."

In my hand I held a dull, old steak knife.

"And with your scissors you snip the cord. It's in your hands. You are now cutting the cord that connects you to your entity."

With the knife I tried to cut the cord, but the opposite happened—the cord cut the knife. The blade grew smaller and smaller until it fell away to nothing, and I was left with an empty plastic handle in my hand. The cord was swollen and hot where the knife rubbed against it.

"And now the cord is cut. I want you to see that the cord is cut, Amanda. I want you to see that you are now free from the entity."

Naamah leapt out of the corner towards me, stopping my heart. The darkness had spread from the corners and now only the center of the room had any light at all, and this a dull dim gray. I saw, without surprise, that the other end of the cord connected to her navel. It dragged on the floor between us.

"Be in your clean, pure space. Feel how good it feels to be free. Be aware of the space inside you where the invader was. We need to fill that hole with healing."

I was full of blood. It came out of my throat and dribbled down my chin. It dripped down onto the floor and slid across the room. The smell was overwhelming.

"And now you're full of the white light of healing. You're a strong, independent person and you can forgive your invader. You can send your entity love and forgiveness, and send it on towards the white light."

Naamah pushed me to the floor of the dark room, now slick with blood, and straddled me.

"Do you forgive me?" she asked.

"And now we're coming awake. We're coming out of our safe, secure place and back into the Ray of Hope Fellowship Headquarters."

My eyes popped open and I saw Ray Thomas standing above me.

"So how did we do, Amanda? Are we feeling free now?"

"Oh yes," I answered, without intent, without my own voice. "I'm so much freer now. This has all been a tremendous learning experience."

THE DEMON wrote a check for $250 and drove back towards the city. Almost there, close to the airport, she stopped at a hotel lounge and made the $250 back having sex with a businessman in the hotel bathroom.

THE NEXT day I saw Dr. Flynn for my last checkup after the rabies shots. The first thing she said was, "How was the beach?"

I hadn't told her we were going to the beach. Nothing could be taken for granted anymore. No one could be trusted.

"You told me," I said, "to eat more salt." The book said that salt enhanced the demon's power.

She smiled. "Yes, how's that working for you?"

"I don't know," I answered. "How was it supposed to work?"

She ignored my question and gave me the shot, still smiling.

"And how was Dr. Fenton?" she asked. "Did he help you figure out your problem?"

"Go to hell," I told her. I got up off the table and walked out, leaving Dr. Flynn smirking behind me.

WHILE WAITING for a train to take me home from the doctor's office, I saw a quick movement, like a jackrabbit, just to my right. I thought I was seeing things. But then the quick white blur rushed by again. Then again and again, zigzagging back and forth. I was sure I was seeing things. No one else looked. But then a small white hand reached out from behind me to knock the book I was reading, *Demon Possession and You*, out of my hand and onto the tracks. I felt her cheek against mine and saw her black hair falling over my shoulder.

"Amanda, why do you make it so hard?"

I TOLD Ed I didn't like Dr. Fenton, but would find another therapist soon. We were sitting at the breakfast table. Ed was reading the paper. "Fine," he said, nodding his head, and quickly went back to the paper. *This is how much you matter to him*, she told me, *a glance up from the paper, no hugs, no kisses, no questions.*

IT ALL started to pick up speed. The joke was on me. Credit cards arrived for me in the mail, sometimes two or three a day. Not the usual schlock that you get, unasked for, like a virus, but high-end, mega-limit gold and platinum cards, a few I had even been rejected for in the past. When I first moved to the city as a teenager I had never even had a checking account before, and it took a few years and many mistakes before I learned how to handle money, which I now did very well. But those stains were still on my record, and as a result the best I could hack was a high-interest secured card with a thousand-dollar limit. Until now. I had no recollection of filling out the applications for these cards—let alone did I know why I had suddenly been approved—but the cards kept rolling in.

The cards were the kind of computer-generated error I could accept without too much trouble, and anyway, I was happy to have them. It was what she did with the cards that was disturbing: she used them. She wanted to shop. New items appeared in my closet daily, never anything I would have chosen myself, but nothing I was entirely unhappy with, either. Perfumes (she liked rich, heavy florals), a new Nepalese rug for the bedroom, crocodile pumps, and an alligator purse. My new credit cards went over their limit. She got more.

WHAT SHE wanted most of all, even more than shopping or cigarettes, was men. The men she wanted were not those whom I would have picked. I had always looked for men with kind sympathy in their faces. Men with soft eyelashes who looked away and acted busy when you caught them staring. Men who didn't fidget with their wedding bands. Naamah, naturally, liked men who hocked their wedding bands in pawn shops. Men who caught your eyes and held them—and then winked. Of course, I only saw them afterwards, when Naamah would leave and I would sink back into consciousness, naked and shivering, in bed with a man I had never seen before.

She didn't hesitate to deal with the men she didn't want, either. I was waiting for a train, on my way back from the Fitzgerald house. It was a little too late to be there, waiting alone for a train. The platform was empty except for myself and one other person, a man. I didn't like the look of him. He had the wrong expression on his face, and a moustache, and the wrong clothes—stained pants and a jacket that was cut-rate ten years ago. He was walking towards me. I wanted to turn around and leave, go back to the token booth and try to call a taxi, but I didn't. Instead I walked towards the man, meeting him halfway.

"Just miss a train?" I heard myself ask. He shrugged. I could not believe I was engaging this man in conversation. He was disgusting up close, with mottled, pitted skin and a shaggy grown out haircut.

"I hate that," I said. "Especially at night. Especially at night when you're waiting for a train and there's someone there. And you never know. I mean, in the city you just never know who you're dealing with. They might have a knife, or a gun, or whatever. They might, I don't know, be the kind of person who hates men who hang out in train stations, waiting for women. She might be the kind of person who takes men like that and rips them limb from fucking limb with her bare hands."

The man left the station without a word, and the train took me home safe and sound.

I n October Ed insisted on having Alex and Sophia over
for dinner—a thank you for the wonderful weekend
at the beach. To tell you something about Sophia, I
had never, in the six years that I knew her, not on one
occasion, seen the soles of her feet. We had spent a week
at the beach with them once, and first thing in the morning she slipped into satin wedge-heeled slippers. On the
boardwalk she wore high-heel clogs; even in the water she
wore cheap plastic thongs. She always wore a black suit,
during the week, and always black high heels—strappy
sandals in the summer, pumps in the spring and fall, tight
curvy boots in the winter. Another thing about Sophia:
she colored her hair (I could tell from the unchanging
shade of baby blonde), but I never once saw her natural
color, not even at the roots, not at her part, not even at
the nape of her neck. I also never saw Sophia gain or
lose a pound, never saw a wrinkle or a pimple or a pore
on her skin, and never saw her sneeze, hiccup, burp, or
fart—although she did occasionally release a dry cough
from her throat. I couldn't stand her.

To tell you something about Alex, after six years I still
knew nothing about him that didn't pertain to either his

career or the fruits of that career—beach house, cars, Claire's private schools. I didn't know where he'd gone to high school, his favorite color, what books or movies or music he loved or hated. I was acutely aware, however, that he was a VP before he was forty and had 30 percent of his retirement income in stocks and the remainder in long-term bonds and real estate.

Ed and I had silently decided to put on a pleasant face for his friends and tell them nothing of our problems. Except that somehow Ed had gotten the idea that I would be cooking dinner, and was shocked, when he got home at six, to find out I had nothing prepared.

"I don't understand," he yelled. "You didn't make ANY-THING? We have people coming over in one hour and you don't even have a box of fucking rice in the house? What the hell am I supposed to serve, cereal and ice cream?"

"No, Ed," I told him. "You mean *you* didn't make any-thing, *you* don't even have a box of rice, and *you* have people coming over in one hour. And no, they can't have my ice cream."

For the first time I couldn't tell who was speaking, me or Naamah.

An hour would have been plenty of time to get some-thing together but we easily killed it fighting and when they got to our place—complaining, as they did with every visit, of how hard our place was to find—we had nothing to serve. Ed confessed that there had been a little mix-up over dinner (he followed this with a revoltingly sycophantic little laugh), and that he'd have to run out and get something. I was beyond even pretending to be amused, and sat sullenly at the kitchen table while Ed babbled. Alex, good sport that he was, went along with Ed for the ride.

Sophia and I were left sitting around the dining table with a bottle of white wine. We both lit cigarettes, the first line of defense against silence and boredom.

"So," I asked her, "what's new?"

"Not much," she said. "We're moving the firm."

"Where are you moving?"

"Just across town. It's just a hassle, that's all. Missing files and everything."

"Moving's a drag."

"Yep."

We smoked and drank our wine. I looked at Sophia, and she was looking at me in an odd way.

"What's different?" she asked.

"What do you mean?"

"You look different. Did you gain a few pounds? It looks good on you. You look healthier."

"No, I don't think so." Of course I knew perfectly well what she was talking about.

"Huh. Well there's *something* different." Sophia was slouching a little in her chair in a typical businessman's posture, legs spread wide. In her right hand was a cigarette and in the other, a glass of wine. Now she put her cigarette out and straightened up in her chair into a stiff, nunlike position, and turned around so she was looking directly at me. I thought she was angry at me. In the corner of my eye I saw something scurry from behind the bedroom door to the bathroom. I was oddly comforted by knowing Naamah was in the room.

"I think," she said from this odd position, "I know what it is."

"What do you mean?"

Out of boredom I had been picking the label off the bottle of wine. Now I looked up at Sophia—and oh, what I saw. Her cheeks bulged out as if she had filled them with air. Her eyes opened wider, and then wider, until they popped almost out of the sockets. Her lips, now thick and engorged with blood, dropped apart to reveal black teeth that shrunk before my eyes into stubby little points.

I drew in a sharp breath with a tiny squeal and jumped out of my chair. In doing so I knocked over the bottle of wine. My eyes darted to the table at the sound of glass hitting wood, and then I blinked, and when I looked back up, Sophia was Sophia again. And she was laughing.

"All I meant," she said, "was that you're looking very good."

I stared at her, speechless.

"Oh, don't be silly," she said with a roll of her eyes. "You're scared. Relax. Soon you'll have the world at your feet."

I said nothing, still frozen. I was just starting to see black, starting to feel myself fade away and the demon rise, when I heard keys rattling by the door. Ed and Alex were back with two shopping bags of take-out Japanese and the laughter of old friends. Naamah slinked back into the shadows, and the rest of the night went on without incident.

THE HORRIBLE thing with Sophia had been so quick that the next day I thought I might have imagined it. Nothing could be taken for granted anymore. Nothing could be assumed.

So I didn't draw any conclusions from what had happened. But a week later another horrible thing happened: I was about to get into a taxi when a woman, a young redhead, appeared in front of me out of nowhere. She stepped right through the door I held open for myself and slammed it behind her. I stared at her through the window, streaked with rain and bright reflections of the streetlights around us. She looked back up at me, laughing, and rolled her eyes up and around in their sockets, revealing a black glistening hole between her eyelids.

Soon after that, during a meeting with a new client at Fields & Carmine, I bent under the table to get a pen that had somehow jumped out of my hand. There under the table, two seats to my right, was the upside-down face of the new client, also bent over, seemingly in search of his errant pen. He caught my eye. I smiled briefly and intended to straighten up again but the demon held me down as strongly as the client's eyes held mine. The client grinned widely, and then wider, stretching his lips across his entire face. He raised his eyebrows up into high pointy peaks until he resembled nothing so much as a clown. "I know you," he mouthed. His throat didn't make a sound but I heard his words clearly in a deep echoing baritone inside my head.

There were more incidents—an odd glance on line at the bank, a quick contorted face across the street—but none as direct as Sophia had been, and I learned nothing from these odd encounters except that there were others, and that I now had the misfortune of being able to see them. Naamah wasn't particularly interested in them, and I wasn't either. By now the most shocking truth wasn't that there were more like her and me, or that her ability to manipulate me was growing so rapidly—it was that, previously, I had been so stupid as to think I had any understanding of the universe at all.

I went back to Sister Maria's. But Maria wouldn't let me in the door. When she saw me through the glass she ran out to the street and stopped me.

"Oh no," she said. "I have children here, my family lives in back. I can't let you in, not like this."

"Like what? What did I do?"

"Amanda, I can see her. She's stronger than ever. Go, get away from here. I tried to help you once already."

I started to cry. "But what am I going to do?" I pleaded.

"Wait here." Maria went back inside, locking the door behind her. She came back with another large glass bottle like the one she had given me before. This one was labeled #17: DEMON BURNING EXTRA STRENGTH.

"And use it this time," she said, slipping it into a brown paper bag. "And there's a book that you need. *Possession*, by K. L. Walker. Now go!"

I STUMBLED away from the store. When I reached a particularly desolate street, lined on either side with weedy lots of burnt cars and old mattresses, I stopped and opened the bag Maria had given me. I opened the bottle and lifted it above my head. I tipped it just a little so that a thin stream trickled onto the crown of my head.

Just then the gray sky split open and fat drops of rain started to fall. I closed my eyes and continued to drip the liquid onto my head. It smelled like anise and musk and ginseng. Through my closed eyes I saw white lightning crack open the sky. My skin stung like a sunburn where the fluid had dripped on it. I opened my eyes to the filthy city street and then I heard laughter. Then I was laughing too, or rather, she was laughing through me. I laughed until I was lying on the filthy concrete, rolling around in yesterday's newspapers and used condoms. I dropped the bottle and it shattered, spilling the potion across the concrete. I rolled in the gutter, wet from rain and bloody from where my skin scraped the concrete and the broken glass. The corners of my mouth started to burn and then crack and bleed, but I kept laughing.

"Amanda," she said through her laughter, our laughter, "did you really think this would work?"

I kept searching for *Possession* by K. L. Walker, the book Maria had told me to read. Missing in every library, sold out in every bookstore. One afternoon I woke up from a blackout to find myself sitting on the floor in front of the mantel. I sat with my legs curled to the side and my face tilted towards the fireplace, as pristine as a girl in a Currier and Ives print. A fire was burning inside it; when my eyes focused and I looked closely I saw a little mountain of books, slowly burning away. As soon as I could, I ran into the kitchen for some water to put out the fire.

Five copies of *Possession*, all burned beyond restoration, the letters of the title just barely visible on the spines.

I gave up on *Possession* and found another book that looked promising—*Demon Warfare Today*—but she knocked it from my hands again. I bought *Protecting Yourself from Evil* but it vanished between the bookstore and the loft. I had put it in my purse, but when I got home it just wasn't there. Soon I found myself unable to even set foot in a bookstore; I would start out with the best intentions and at the door I would find myself turning away, never able to open the door. I would end up getting

an ice cream from a street vendor or stealing another lipstick from a drugstore. The same thing happened if I tried
to enter a church, or a synagogue, or even the Society for
Ethical Culture, as I tried one bright fall afternoon. Even
if I had had the capacity to schedule and keep an appointment with a therapist, I wouldn't have gone. I was sure
that there was no one I could trust.

The battle was all mine, and I was quickly, obviously,
losing.

S oon I didn't have a moment alone. When she wasn't inside me, I could see her scurrying around, looking over my shoulder, ready to jump in if necessary. In the apartment I would see a lock of dirty black hair or a small white foot hiding in the shadows out of the corner of my eye. At the office I would catch sight of her hand, with its long unpolished nails, scribbling alterations over my designs.

Blackouts became common. Ten minutes on the way home from work, an hour, then two or three, then whole days. Ed's birthday came and went and I didn't remember a moment of it. Apparently it didn't go well—the next day he wasn't speaking to me.

Most of the time I was in between the two extremes. I would start a thought—"I really ought to let this person merge in front of me"—and she would finish it—"but why should I?" Or she would start—"We won't go to work today. Instead, I think, we'll get dressed up and go back to that little bar where the bartender had those strong legs." I would scream and cry and beg and fight every way I could imagine, but she would always win. She was stronger, and so she always won.

My new psychic vision, which had seemed like nothing more than a clever parlor trick before, started to turn on me. In early November I was in the Fitzgerald house alone, double-checking the measurements of a wall where a closet would go. I was on the third floor, measuring, when I noticed a dark brown stain on the plaster, one big splash surrounded by an increasingly finer spray. It looked like blood. I tried to avoid the marks but while pulling a tape measure across the wall I couldn't help brushing the side of my hand lightly against a splatter of the stain. The dry skin on the side of my hand, under my smallest finger, barely brushed against the smallest dots of the stain.

When my hand met with the cold wall the world stopped. It all stopped and was instantly replaced with another world. Same room, but it was crowded with cheap, fading clothes. The air was hot and smelled like dirty laundry and cigarette butts. Summertime.

The room was quiet except for the grunts and footsteps of two men grappling in what looked like an equal struggle. The two were of similar size and shape and looked alike. Both were black, of medium build, and dressed in cheap pants and sweat-soaked shirts with wide collars. I couldn't see their faces clearly but their backs looked alike. They could have been brothers.

The man closer to me had something shiny in his right hand. I focused on his hand and my vision zoomed in, like a camera. It was a small knife, an open penknife with a black textured handle. In one lightning-quick motion he freed his right arm from the other man's grip, drew his arm back, and stabbed his brother in the side of the neck. The dying man fell against the wall, where his blood shot out against the plaster and sprayed to where my hand had touched . . .

And then it was over. I was back in the empty, quiet room. I let out a little yelp, ran out of the house, ran to my car, and drove away as quickly as I could.

It didn't end there. The Chinese vanity I had loved so much now had to go. Each time I touched it I was overwhelmed with a flood of sadness that the previous owner had left behind. He was a miserable little man, an antique dealer living alone in the back of his shop, whose main occupation was buying and reading porn. I traded the wardrobe for a plain Shaker-style dresser which carried no emotions at all, just a general sense of industry. A vintage yellow dress I had saved for special occasions now made me nauseated—its previous owner had been a drunk, and when I wore it I felt my liver burn with cirrhosis.

*

ON THE first day of December I set out to buy Ed a Christmas present. Over the summer he had admired a little silver salt bowl in a ridiculously overpriced shop uptown, and I wanted to see if it was still there before I bought another blue sweater.

I was amazed at how quickly we'd fallen apart after the weekend at the beach. Even peaceful moments were glazed over with anger and resentment. No more laughing at bad movies. No more pet names. No more talking in our own secret code. Our time together was all very formal now.

"Are you going to the store?"

"Yep. You want something?"

"Can you pick me up some orange juice? The one—"

"Yeah, I know. Sure."

"Thank you."

"No problem."

I was walking down a quiet, tree-lined street on my way to the store. The air was cold and dry even though the sun was bright. On either side of me were the huge gingerbread limestone and marble houses that made the neighborhood famous. Most of them were apartment buildings now, or private schools. I walked and day-dreamed. She would leave me, eventually. She would grow sick of me, get tired of the fighting, and leave me alone. I would finally be able to tell Ed the truth and he would have to forgive me.

A door to my right opened up and a crowd of girls

poured out, nine or ten years old; each seemed to have the same fine creamy skin, and thick hair held back in a ponytail. A few were wrapped in scarves and gloves and earmuffs, but most wore their coats open. I stopped to let them go. I wasn't in a hurry. I lit a cigarette and watched the girls pass. Behind the crowd were two women—teachers, I guessed. They looked at me pointedly. Just doing their jobs, I thought, the girls were their commodity, to be guarded with their lives. One of the girls was running in my direction, to catch a bus or an afterschool dance class, and she turned her head around to call to a friend—"Call me tonight! Don't forget!"—and ran right into me. I grabbed her elbows to keep her from falling. She was momentarily stunned.

"I'm sorry!" she said. She was a brunette with a worried look on her little face. It was clear she expected a talking-to. I let go of her elbows and gave her a smile.

"Don't worry," I told her. "No harm done."

She smiled with relief and went running on her way. To my left I saw Naamah's shadow, standing behind me.

The crowd of girls thinned out and I went on. But further down the block I was hit again, this time by a woman a little older than me, barreling down the street in such a hurry I couldn't jump out of her way quickly enough. She stumbled a bit when she ran into me, and I took her arm to steady her. Her blonde hair was crisply fluffed around her face and over her forehead, arranged to hide her wrinkles.

"Excuse *me*," she said, cold and sarcastic. She tried to pull her arm back. I wanted to let go of her wrist. I wasn't that angry. But my hand wouldn't comply.

"You shouldn't talk to strangers," I told her. "You should look both ways before you cross the street." My eyes shifted out of focus and the world turned a hazy black streaked with red as I heard myself speak.

Finally the words slowed to a stop and the haze cleared back into focus. The woman lay on the ground, sobbing. I had snapped her wrist in two.

I TRIED to tell Edward. I tried to tell anyone who would listen. But now, I found, it was too late. I opened my mouth to speak and the wrong words came out. *Edward, help me*, became *Edward, pass the salt. I'm possessed* turned into *I'm tired*.

I tried to catch her off guard, to scream out the truth at an unexpected moment. But you can't surprise a thing that lives inside you. The screams came out of my throat as long, dry coughs. *Help me*, I was screaming inside, *save me*—but all anyone heard was a long *ahem*.

Each day I would wake up and say to myself: Today, no more of this nonsense. Today I am going to put all this craziness behind me and be a normal human being.

And she would answer: *But I love you, Amanda. I love you and I'm never leaving.*

Go! I would silently scream at her. *Get out!*

Oh no, she would answer, *I'm not going anywhere.*

Then, first thing, she would start a fight with Ed. He would say "Good morning" and I would try to say "Good morning" back and nothing would come out. I would struggle and twist and try to use my vocal cords to speak and I couldn't. My throat was hers now. So I would say nothing at all. "Well *someone*'s in a good mood," he would say, eyebrows raised. Or maybe after "Good morning" she would say "What's so fucking good about it?" or "Why isn't there more coffee?" or—and this was the worst—she would say "Good morning" back, the words so swampy with sarcasm that Ed would slam down his coffee and leave for work without saying good-bye.

E very night now, after I fell asleep, she took me to
the crimson beach by the red sea.
"Why," I asked her. "Why me?"

"Why not you," she answered. "Who would be better?"

I couldn't answer that. "I don't know what you want,"
I told her. "Tell me. I'll give you anything, whatever you
want."

"All I want is you," she said. "I can't have fun without
you."

"What do you want?" I begged. "What fun?"

"This."

WE WERE back on solid ground, in a big glistening room
with thousands of tiny lights. Chandeliers. A party. Black
tie. The noise of the party was a steady, faraway roar.

I was standing by the bar, one finger tracing the neck-
line of my dress. It looked like me, it was me, but it was
her. I was dressed perfectly. Black dress, sheer hose, shiny
spike heels. I felt a thick coating of makeup on my face
and a strain on my scalp where my hair was pulled into
an upsweep.

There was a tap on my shoulder. I turned around; a

man stood behind us, smiling. He was young and blond with a big smile. In his tuxedo he looked almost like a boy playing dress up.

"I thought you were meeting me on the dance floor," he said.

I shrugged. "I don't feel like dancing. Why don't we go for a walk instead?"

"Where to?"

"Around." I took his hand and led him across the big room to a little hallway hidden behind the dance floor. We walked; the hall got darker and the wallpaper ended and the carpet stopped. The sounds of the party were gone. We walked down a short flight of stairs to a concrete basement. The mechanisms supporting the party were hidden here—a walk-in freezer, a boiler, pipes that led from one mystery to another. The room was lit by a few bare bulbs.

"What are we doing here?" he finally asked. He smiled again but the smile was now a little nervous, a little forced. He was scared. I stepped towards him and kissed him, and he relaxed into my arms. While we kissed I began to take off his clothes: first the jacket, then the tie, then the shirt. The skin on his back was perfectly warm and smooth. I was lost in his skin and his lips, against the back of my eyes I saw a deep dark red. I was running my nails hard over his back, biting his lip, his tongue. He tried to push me away but he couldn't, I was too strong. Blood was trickling down his chin from his lip. He tried to scream but I muffled it with my mouth. I dug my nails deep into his back until the perfect skin was ripped. He tried to get hold of my arms, tried to do something, anything, but Naamah was stronger. She was bringing one hand up to his neck when we were interrupted.

"Hey!" we heard from the top of the stairs. "Who's down there? Come back up, no one's allowed—"

I dropped him and ran.

WE WERE back on the red beach. Crimson fish jumped in and out of the ocean. The wind blew my hair around my face.

"Why?" I asked her again.

"Why, why why?" She was making fun of me. "You know why, Amanda. You let me in. You invited me."

"You're LYING," I screamed. "I never wanted any of this."

"Look!" she pointed to the horizon. Across the sky a scene was played out. It was me and Ed in the loft, the night I burned him with a cigarette. We sat on the sofa, I moved my arm to put out my cigarette, and just like I remembered, my right arm made a quick turn to stick Ed in the leg with it. He screamed. I screamed. And then the vision froze. In that split second after the scream, a quick, small smile flashed across my face. I was glad, glad because Ed deserved it, that and worse.

"You made me!" I screamed. "You made me do it and you made me like it! All of it."

Naamah sighed, clearly impatient. "I never made you do anything," she said. "I only let you do what you wanted. I told you, Amanda, I can't have fun without you."

My performance at work started to slip. I came in late, I left early, I often skipped important meetings altogether. The work that I did do was creatively brilliant but technically sloppy. The demon had no mind for specifics—she didn't even care if a design was physically possible, for that matter, as long as it was pretty. My coworkers grumbled but I had been well liked before. Everyone, I imagined, wanted to give me another chance.

Everyone except James Cronin. He went to Leon Fields and John Carmine, ratted me out on the few shortcomings they hadn't yet noticed, and got himself placed in charge of the Fitzgerald house.

Nothing happened for the first week. And the second went off fine. But halfway through the third I was not surprised to find myself at the office late one night, asking him out for a drink.

We were alone in the office. James, Naamah, and me. He was sitting at his desk and I was standing next to him, unclear of how I had arranged for us to be there. Most of the lights were off. Only the one fluorescent fixture above his desk shone down on us, casting the room beyond into shadow.

"How about a drink," I heard her ask.

"Huh?" James asked.

"Come on," she said. "One drink. I'm not ready to go home yet." I felt my lips turn up. One eyebrow arched and my head tilted slightly toward the right.

"Sure. Why not?" He stood up and reached for his coat. Then the edges of my vision turned darker and darker until I was seeing through a pinhole, and before we were out the door everything was black and I wasn't, I no longer was . . .

And then I was back. A horrible smell, years of urine and decay. Darkness. After a moment my eyes adjusted and I saw that I was outdoors, in an alley. No, not an alley, but a tunnel. I turned around. The tunnel was about fifty feet long and ten feet wide, with a dim light at either end. Under the smell of piss was another smell, familiar, a mix of grass and dirt and shit. The park. I was in a tunnel under a hill in a city park.

I was standing above James Cronin's body. He was lying on his back. His neck was bent so his head was parallel to his shoulders and behind it I could see a thick pool of blood.

I stepped over James and walked ten feet south. Aside from my footsteps the tunnel was silent. Along the wall were the remains of an old water fountain, a stunning mosaic of Medusa, snakes coiling from her head; in better days water would have flowed from her mouth. Her eyes looked at me with complete understanding. I had always loved that fountain.

I walked back to where James lay and crouched down to look at him. Of course he hadn't moved. His jacket was open and the top of his pants was undone. He had probably been promised a little lurid semipublic fun. His face looked like it always did; even dead he looked smug.

There was nothing I could do. So I stood up, walked out of the tunnel, walked through the park to the streets of the city, and then hailed a taxi to take me back home.

JAMES, NATURALLY, didn't come to work the next day or call in sick. At lunchtime a collective anxiety began to swell in the office. It wasn't like James not to show up. It wasn't like James not to call. A few people left messages on his answering machine. *James, we just want to know if you're okay. James, we're worried—please call the office.* The anxiety grew and by four o'clock we were asking each other, does James have a girlfriend? Do you know any of his friends, relatives? Well, it's just one day, we reassured each other. Just a day. If he's not in tomorrow, we'll do something. No one knew what, exactly, we would do, but we were quite sure if he wasn't in tomorrow we would take action.

At lunchtime the next day Ginny McPhee called the police. Alex Levaux told her she was overreacting.

"I don't care," she said sharply. "It's wrong, to sit here and do nothing when James could be in the hospital or sick or something."

Two officers in blue uniforms came. Ginny gave them

the general lowdown. They asked the questions you would expect, each one irrelevant. Was James a drug addict? Alcoholic? Gambler? Did he owe anyone money? I listened from my desk nearby.

The anxiety built to a crescendo when Ginny McPhee phoned the police again the next morning and was told that James was now officially missing. Fields & Carmine called his family in Ohio. Ginny checked in with the police every day. No leads, no evidence, no clues. Then something happened at Fields & Carmine I wouldn't have expected—we got used to it. We stopped talking about it. Stopped thinking about it. The office settled into a new pattern, a pattern where James was gone and that was that. Like the good stapler that was on your desk every morning for years, the best one that never jammed, and then one day it was gone. You spent a few days poking around for it and then you got a new one, and went on with your life, and accepted the disappearance as one of life's little mysteries, never solved. That's what we did with James.

Except Ginny McPhee. She cried at her desk. She talked about him all the time. She called the police every day until they finally had an answer, two weeks after his death: James had been mugged and killed in the park after leaving work on Tuesday. His body had been found the next morning but there had been a little mix-up with the ID. It was unlikely that the man who did it could be caught this long after the fact. So unlikely that the police made it perfectly clear it wasn't worth putting a lot of time and money into the thing. Fields & Carmine closed the office for the rest of the week and on Sunday we all cried at his funeral. Then on Monday we all went back to work and settled back into a new routine, a routine where one of our coworkers was dead, and that was the end of James Cronin.

SOON AFTER that I stopped going to work. I don't know if I gave notice or just stopped going, only that I never found myself at Fields & Carmine anymore. Ed had no idea. In better days he had called me at work twice a day but it was months now since either of us had called just to hear the other's voice and say hello. By the time he even knew I had lost my job, it was the least of our concerns.

AGAIN, I found myself in the dark little bar around the corner from what used to be my office. Again, I was sitting with the same man—handsome, tattooed, drunk.

"Eric," I said. I didn't know how I had gotten here or how I knew his name, but here I was.

"Naamah," he said. "That's a weird one. What's that, Arabic?"

"Satanic," I answered.

"Huh?"

"Akashic."

"What's that, like Persian?"

"Oh yes."

"Huh. So, are we going?"

"Going?"

"For a ride. You said you wanted to go for a ride."

"Right," I said. "I'm coming. We're going."

C hristmas and New Year's came and went. I missed them entirely. The days were short and cold and the nights far too long. Ed stopped asking where I had been. No longer expected me home for dinner, no longer responded when Naamah tried to pick her little fights. He was at the end of his rope now. He had tried kindness, understanding, suggestions, attempts at therapy, he had yelled at me, he had pleaded, ignored, and now, finally, he was going on with his life.

The tables started to turn, and Edward was the one picking the fights. He was the one late for dinner, and then late for bed, and then home late, late, into the night.

The proof was a phone call. He thought I was out, not surprisingly. We'd given up keeping track of each other's whereabouts, and I wasn't usually home in the evenings anymore. But that night I was in the bedroom. The demon was doing something with the herbs she kept buried in my lingerie drawer. The little bundles of twigs and roots had started showing up a few weeks ago. What she did with them, I was never quite sure, but the time the demon spent at home was often spent with them, burning a little pile in an ashtray or rearranging the bundles into different combinations. Luckily the demon was interested in what Ed was saying and so she took me closer to the wall to listen. He was on the phone with someone.

"No. I don't know. I don't think she's going to the doctor anymore." A pause for the woman on the other end to answer. "I don't know what I'm going to do. No, not tonight, I'm already home. Tomorrow . . . Yeah, I know. It has to change . . . Of course I tried talking to her, I tried a million times. Look, just drop it, okay . . . No, I really don't want to talk about it. Tomorrow. Tomorrow . . . All right, good night . . . I love you, too."

Edward hung up the phone, and the demon went back to playing with her herbs.

SOON ED was spending whole weekends out of the house. He made vague claims about business trips that neither of us pretended to believe. When he was home, he slept on the couch. We used chilly exaggerated "pleases" and "thank yous" with each other. If one of our limbs were to brush against the other person's it was immediately retracted and stiffened.

On his last day at home, Ed found me in bed with another man. The man had come to read the gas meter, apparently, and I couldn't say for sure what happened after that. When Ed came home, the man got up, got dressed, and scurried out of the building so quickly I didn't see him go.

Edward left me right then and there.

148

I lay on the bed, still naked, and cried silently to myself. Ed pulled out a brown leather suitcase I had never seen before and started packing. Even now I can't stop thinking about that suitcase. Was he waiting for this occasion? Did his girlfriend buy it for him?

He spoke the whole time that he packed, throwing as many clothes around the room as into the suitcase. Through the demon's filter I heard only snatches of words and phrases.

"I knew it . . . I fucking knew it . . . Bullshit . . . Responsibility . . . Refuse to take responsibility . . . Refuse to talk about it . . . "

Edward threw a shoe across the room. I felt my lips bend into a smile. I rolled back and forth on the bed and I heard myself laughing. The demon was hysterical, ecstatic. She wanted him gone. The last thing I remember from that day is Edward kneeling by the bed, trying to get me to focus on his words.

"Amanda, are you listening? Amanda this is TOO MUCH. I'm leaving. Amanda, do you hear me? I'M LEAVING!"

WITH ED gone, time slipped away from me. I would wake up from a blackout thinking an hour or two had passed to find out days had gone by. Occasional slices of consciousness blended into each other and I was left with a string of non sequiturs.

I was in a bed, on a huge round mattress with the softest sheets I've ever felt. The walls were sky blue with white rococo trim around the top. It reminded me of the Fitzgerald house. The room was huge, almost as big as the loft. It was maybe the biggest room I'd ever seen. I was naked and alone. And then the blackness drowned out my eyes and ears and the rest of me and I was gone.

Out of the blue room. Back in the loft. I was sitting in front of the fireplace, methodically burning each item of Ed's clothing. There was a knock at the door. No, a knock on *a* door. From the inside of the bathroom. The immense dining-room table had been moved in front of the bathroom to keep someone in.

"Please," a woman was crying out. "I'll do anything, just please let me out. I need a doctor. I've been hurt."

"Oh no," Naamah answered. "I don't think you're done yet."

Pink. Lots of pink. Slowly I saw I was in a woman's bedroom. No, a lingerie shop. Everything was pink and gold. The type of store found in every upscale mall and shopping district in the country. I could have been anywhere. Thin notes of classical music streamed through the aisles of wiry bras and flimsy negligees. I was walking down a long rack of bras, pulling out a lacy number every few feet. With a jagged, chipped fingernail on the index finger of my right hand I tore into the softest part of each little confection. *Rrrrrrrrrip* into white lace, red satin, black sheer nylon. *Rrrrrrrrrip*; a yellow underwire makes a particularly satisfying little sound. I walked the rest of the aisle and then back up the other side, singling out every fourth or fifth bra for a nice deep *rrrrip*.

Days later. All around me was grayness and a sour smell. On a train. The car was half full. A few men in sorry, sagging suits, women with too many children. I looked down; I was wearing a black dress I'd never seen before, buttoned down the front, very nice, and an equally mysterious pair of white leather pumps. Eyes. I felt a pair of furtive eyes darting up at us and then away, up and then away. I looked up; across the car I saw a dirty, rat-faced young woman, twenty at the oldest, watching me with a repulsive, knowing smirk. Greasy dark hair fell straight down from her scalp to the top of her shoulders. She wore a grimy denim jacket and underneath that a black top with the name of a death metal band on it. Her dishwater eyes shone. The rat face glanced around to make sure no one was watching and then turned back to give me her full attention. Then she stuck out her tongue, wide and flat, straight down to her chin. The top half of her body leaned backwards and her tongue slowly curled up towards her nose. For all the world she looked like a snake charmer with a wide, pink snake. The pink snake stretched to the tip of her nose, past the bridge, and then up to rest its tip in between her eyebrows. To my horror—and to Naamah's great amusement—the girl, with the blue underside of her tongue covering half of her face, leaned back even further, so her head was facing the ceiling, and her eyes rolled back to show only the whites.

From under her tongue came a little black cloud that smelled like blood. I watched in awe as the cloud floated towards my mouth. When it was close enough Naamah opened her mouth, leaned towards the cloud, and ate it right out of the air, as easy as a frog swallowing a fly.

I woke up on a street corner not far from home, vomiting into a trash can.

"Miss? Excuse me, miss."

I looked up to see a police officer standing in front of me, a burly mustached beefcake of a man trying to peek down my shirt. He offered me a ride home. I gratefully accepted. In the back of the squad car the doors didn't have latches. A thick divider of plastic separated the front seat from the back—or would have if the officer had shut it.

They always trust a pretty face.

And then the officer said, "The wife's got it too. The stomach flu. Last week the kids had it, now my mother's coming down with it. It's a killer, this virus, it's a fucking killer and they all got it."

He paused and looked in the rearview mirror, where he saw me staring at him. He cleared his throat and adjusted his hat on his head.

"Excuse me," he said. "I apologize. What I mean is, the flu is a terrible thing."

WE WERE back on the red beach by the crimson sea. Now I knew that the sea was blood, and it had stained the sand. She dipped in and out of the ocean, as sleek and happy as a dolphin.

I turned and tried to run. But it was as if I were the one who was underwater, I couldn't gather the momentum to move my arms and legs. And then she was right next to me, standing on the beach, smiling to show her small pointed teeth, watching me try to run.

"Amanda," she said, "stop trying. I love you. I'm never letting you go."

A nd then one day, during a long white snowstorm, Ed came home. The demon had brought me back to the apartment after days of her kind of fun and there he was, sitting on the sofa in a rumpled suit and tie, a little puddle of melted snow around his feet. For the first time in weeks I found my own voice.

"Ed," I cried. I ran to him, to his sad, aged face, and sat down close and put my arms around him. He stayed still and tense in his forward-facing position but I didn't mind. Just to see him again was more than I had hoped for. After a quick moment of having him in my arms he pulled away and stood up. He paced awkwardly in front of the sofa, looking out the windows, towards the door, anywhere but at me.

"I tried to call," he said. "I wrote. You never answered. I thought maybe you'd moved. I, I,—"

He started to cry. He fought it at first, said "I" a few more times in a strangled, choked voice and then admitted he was crying, let his face crumple and tears pour down and his nose run as he paced. My heart leapt. Maybe there was a way, I thought, I could explain and—

"Oh Ed, I—" *I love you*, I wanted to say. *I love you and*

I miss you and I don't know why this happened. To us, out of everyone in the world. Remember the flowers you gave me on our third date? Remember the seagulls we laughed at on the beach last year? The horrible movie, the one with the subtitles, we made jokes about for weeks. Long Saturdays in the park. Sundays at the flea market. The Christmas party where we drank so much and got in a huge fight and almost killed each other, the next day it was so funny. The candy you bought me when you didn't come home. It's not fair. It's not fair. But Naamah locked my throat closed and I sat poker-faced as he pulled himself together.

"I'm filing for a divorce," he said. "I want to get married again."

All the nights I waited. The nights you never called.

"I'm sure it's not a surprise. It's been over a year. She—well, I know you know. We both—there's no point in getting into it. I don't know why we could never talk about it, we could have done this so much sooner, we could have both gone on . . . "

The rooftop pool in California where we watched the sunset. All the take-out meals. The feel of your skin warm and dry against mine. Your mother's birthday parties. Your father's funeral. We were going to go to Hawaii someday, to Paris someday. We were going to buy a new dishwasher, a new car. Nothing's changed, I wanted to say, *not for me, I'm still here, look at me, look at me*—but when I tried to open my mouth I couldn't. I was falling, down into the thick red haze, an endless black well, I clung and grasped with all my might, I wanted to stay, but there was nothing to cling to, nothing to grab, and I fell and fell until I was gone.

I was lying on the crimson sand by the blood red sea. Naamah lay next to me. She smiled and in the sand she wrote two words with her left index finger: I WIN.

First was Lilith. She was Adam's first wife but she wasn't good enough at all, she wouldn't lie down and take it and she wouldn't do what she was asked or told. So I was made to order. Everything would be in place. Everything would be just so. There wouldn't be any mistakes, this time, and so on the new wild earth he watched while I was made from a handful of clean dust. First were the bones. He started with the feet and then up the legs to the hips, spine, and ribs, out for the arms, and then the white round skull on top. Next was what I needed to live—liver, spleen, bowels, uterus, heart and lungs, brain, eyes and tongue, all made from dust before my partner's eyes. Then the muscles were layered on, then the fascia, the meridians, the tendons, and the veins. I was filled with blood, bile, mucus, tears. And then I was wrapped in skin and sprinkled with hair and the new lids on my eyes rolled up and the irises rolled down and, now complete and real, I saw my partner, alone in the world with me.

My first sight was his face twisted with disgust, before he quickly turned away. He was disgusted by me, and begged never to have to look at me again. Because he had

159

never known what was inside before. He had imagined a person was as sleek and neat on the inside as outside. He couldn't stand the mess, the chaos, the blood.

I wasn't needed. I wasn't wanted. But Lilith taught me a few tricks on the banks of the Red Sea. When Adam refused to sleep with Eve, horrified that Cain had killed Abel, I came to him in his sleep. He thought it was a dream, but he was the father of my first child.

They can't say no. All I need is a way in. A dream is the easy way but then they never know, they never even know I had them. I need someone like Amanda. She says she didn't know. She says she didn't want me. But I couldn't have gotten in if she didn't want me. Everyone wanted me. Each and every one.

Everyone except Ed.

T hen I was sitting on the sofa in our apartment. Through the windows I saw a wall of white snow falling down. People were everywhere, all of them moving, walking from one room to another and back again. Two were snapping photos, a few more were looking through the apartment, poking under the table and in the bookcases. A strange kind of party. A man took my picture; I shuddered at the bright light. When my eyes cleared I looked toward the open door of the bedroom. Where was Ed?

My hearing faded back in. At first all I heard was a general buzz, the chatter of the party, and then one voice singled itself out. A man was talking to me, yelling almost, right in my ear. I turned my head. The man was sitting next to me on the sofa, an older man with slicked back hair and a cheap suit, talking loudly at me.

"Why did you DO IT? Were you having AN AFFAIR? Did he GAMBLE? Did he DRINK?"

Shhh, I tried to tell him, you don't have to yell, but the words came out garbled and fuzzy; my mouth wasn't all mine again yet. I looked down and saw a stain on my dress, a big red wet stain on my abdomen. I'm bleeding,

I tried to tell the man. He watched me carefully as I unbuttoned my jacket and then my shirt. Everyone was watching but if I was bleeding to death, I thought, I certainly ought to be able to see the wound. But after my shirt was undone and my stomach was bare there was no red. It wasn't me who was bleeding.

"Ed," I screamed. I jumped up off the sofa. "Edward!" Everyone in the room stopped moving and looked at me.

"Where is he?" I screamed.

No one answered. They stood still around me and watched as I ran to the bathroom, which was empty, then to the kitchen, also empty, and then to the bedroom.

In the bedroom, blood was everywhere. Splattered on the walls, smeared on the floor. The bed was soaked through with it. On the white cotton sheets we had picked out together last year. On the goose down pillows Ed's mother had given us two years ago for Christmas. On the black-and-white quilt we'd found at a flea market upstate, one beautiful sunny Saturday three years before. The smell was sickening. I closed my eyes and wished it all away, but when I opened them again nothing had changed. The man with slicked back hair stood next to me again.

"Why did you DO IT? Why did you KILL him?"

I moaned and vomited on the floor. When I held my head back up I saw, finger-painted in browning crimson on the white wall above the bed:

I WIN.

*

SOMEONE IN the building, I guess, called the police. His screams must have been unbearably loud—our nearest neighbor was two stories down. With the assistance of a public defender, who was obviously terrified of me, I pleaded to insanity and agreed to indefinite incarceration in a psychiatric hospital.

First I stabbed a girl with one of those homemade knives. I don't know why. Then, in solitary, I grew my nails long and attacked one of the guards. Lucky for her she wasn't pretty to begin with. So I got moved to high security.

She has a grand old time here, she has all the girls following her orders, she's sleeping with one of the guards and maybe one of the doctors. She's like a fox in a chicken coop here in the hospital.

When I have a rare moment to myself, I lie in bed and think about Edward. I try to think of the good times, about how beautiful he was, his blond hair falling over his eyes just so when he smiled. And our home, our great big beautiful loft. I try to hold on to every last inch of him; his hands with the always-perfect square nails, thin gold band around his third finger; the soft curve where his neck dipped into his chest, and then rose to meet his collarbone; the way he liked everything just so; he would be so pleased when the apartment was clean and everything was in its place.

But as much as I try, mostly what I remember is the bedroom filled with blood.

O *f course she fought at first. They all do. And then* *they see the possibilities and they're happy to go* *along. She could have gone on forever, in her* *small lonely life. But sometimes the door to a bigger life* *opens, and it isn't so easy to say No. You can't spend your* *whole life saying No. Sometimes you have to say Yes, and* *see where it takes you.*

I'M HERS all the time now, and when I see a small slice of the world it's through her eyes, which used to be mine. Once, some time ago, I caught sight of myself in a mirror. I looked so different, older, but really more beautiful. My hair was thick and it was longer than before, and my skin was creamy and smooth. At night she takes me to the crimson beach by the red sea and we lie down and she wraps her arms around me. She tells me I'm beautiful, that she still loves me as much as she ever did, that she still wants us to be friends.

"I'll never leave you," she tells me, and she jabs with her tongue. "I love you," she tells me, "I'll never leave you alone." And that's all I've ever wanted, really: someone to love me, and never leave me alone.